PUT THE SKY
INSIDE OF YOU

———— MILOS TOTH ————

authorHOUSE®

AuthorHouse™
1663 Liberty Drive
Bloomington, IN 47403
www.authorhouse.com
Phone: 1 (800) 839-8640

Published by AuthorHouse   09/22/2016

ISBN: 978-1-5246-4105-4 (sc)
ISBN: 978-1-5246-4103-0 (hc)
ISBN: 978-1-5246-4104-7 (e)

Library of Congress Control Number: 2016915676

Print information available on the last page.

Any people depicted in stock imagery provided by Thinkstock are models,
and such images are being used for illustrative purposes only.
Certain stock imagery © Thinkstock.

This book is printed on acid-free paper.

Because of the dynamic nature of the Internet, any web addresses or links contained in
this book may have changed since publication and may no longer be valid. The views
expressed in this work are solely those of the author and do not necessarily reflect the
views of the publisher, and the publisher hereby disclaims any responsibility for them.

Scripture quotations marked NIV are taken from the Holy Bible, New
International Version®. NIV®. Copyright © 1973, 1978, 1984 by International
Bible Society. Used by permission of Zondervan. All rights reserved.

PUT THE SKY INSIDE OF YOU

If you are desperate, if you think you don't know how to live,
And you don't know what to do
Put the sky inside of you

Contents

Acknowledgements

My thanks belong to Stephanie Kemp for editing work and her inputs that significantly contributed to the final version of this manuscript.

I would also like to thank Monica Gabriny Rokus for designing the cover for this book and her encouragement to publish the book.

This Book is dedicated to **Pavla, Victoria, Natalie**

Chapter 1: Love is behind that jump

In the year of 413 BC there was a request by Socrates to gather all the famous philosophers of that time in Athens, Greece to dine and discuss the question: "What is Love?" The request was sent by human courier since there were no computers at that time and not even a postal mail service. In the request Socrates wrote: "Dear fellow philosophers, please attend the dinner which will be held at my residence in Athens on September 28th. After eating and drinking we will discuss one of the most puzzling human feelings: Love. I can't figure out on my own what love is, why human beings possess such a feeling and what kind of spark ignites the love. I hope that if all of us—the smartest people on the earth—put our heads together we come up with the answer."

The day of the gathering was a Saturday. Some philosophers took several days to get to Athens. Some of them travelled on horses, some on mules, some walked. After they ate dinner, drank wine they started to debate. One would think that Socrates would come up with the greatest idea and explain to everybody else What Love is. But it was Aristophanes who came with the most interesting explanation: "In the beginning of time people did not exist in single bodies as we do now but, rather, were pairs joined at the shoulders. There were three types of pairs: male-female, male-male, and female-female. These twin-type creatures tumbled around all day, carefree and, of course, never lonely. Zeus, father of Gods and men, like the twin-type people; however, one day, (nobody knows why) twin-type people offended Zeus so much that Zeus cut them in half as a punishment. Afterward, they walked around lonely, searching endlessly for their other half. And so it is to this day that human beings wander through life looking for the person who will complete them, for in our true and original nature, we were not one but two." Aristophanes finished his input to the debate. The other philosophers listened calmly and nodded with agreement...

Chapter 2: Mandatory army serving time

Czechoslovakia was a socialist country back in the 1980s. There was a mandatory requirement for all male adults aged 18 and older to serve in an army for two years. Two years locked in the camp called a '*kasarne*'. Kasarne: a military training ground with a set of buildings surrounded by a big concrete-panel fence so the soldiers could not escape. Some young fellows figured out how to avoid the two-year service. They simulated some illness, or bribed an army bureaucrat who then signed a special type of document excusing them from the two years of a military service.

Jozef had to serve for just one year because young men who finished University didn't have to serve for two years; they had to serve for one year only. During the last two years of their five years of graduate studies they had mandatory army classes one day of every week, which then was counted as one year towards their mandatory military service.

The boys aged 19, 20, 21, 22 (rarely older) were locked in the *kasarne*. Most of them felt deprived of their youth, deprived of chatting with girls, deprived of having the fun that an ordinary free life would otherwise offer to them. They could go out of the *kasarne* to the town in which they were serving their "two year sentences" once or twice a week for couple of hours. They were also allowed once or twice in a year to go to their home-town (which was usually far away) for just a couple of days. When they were out of the *kasarne* in public they still had to wear army uniforms so everybody could recognize them. Girls in the town quite often avoided the young soldiers. They kind of knew that the guys were missing something and the guys would most likely make trouble for them.

Jozef enjoyed one year of the serving in the military. He had been assigned to check the airplane jet fighters before the fighter flew its missions. His *kasarne* was located in the Czech town of Hradec Kralove (around 150 km east of Prague). During his free time—when Jozef was not checking the jet fighters or participating in flying missions—he either worked out, played ping-pong or chess, read books, cut the hair of other soldiers or wrote letters.

There were nine soldiers, including Jozef, sharing one room. They considered themselves to be the lucky ones. In other rooms there were 20-30 beds for the same number of soldiers. One of the other nine-member room crew was Jirka, born and raised in Prague. Jirka noticed that Jozef was often writing something. He also noticed that when Jozef was writing he used carbon paper to retain copies of his writing.

One day Jirka asked, "Jozef, would you write a letter for me?"

"What kind of letter you want me to write Jirko?" Jozef used Jirka's name variation.

"You know," Jirka said, "I like one girl very much. I am thinking to write her something. I don't know what. I have never written a letter to a girl."

Jozef looked up at Jirka; Jirka was smiling.

"So you want me to write something for her?" asked Jozef.

"Yes," Jirka replied, "would you do that?"

"Piece of cake, Jirka. Describe to me the girl you are talking about, so I have some kind of idea what to write... you know what Jirka? You don't have to tell me anything about that girl, let me write something; then I will let your read it and you tell me whether you like it or not, and if you like it you can send that letter to her."

Jirka nodded in agreement, grinning.

Jozef started to write:

> *Dear young lady,*
> *The first time I saw you sitting on the steps in Vaclav Square next to the statue of King Vaclav sitting on a horse, a thought came through my mind: 'that girl is so beautiful. She sits so gracefully. I have to do something... I don't what, but I will figure it out'. That was the thought when I first saw you. Then later on I knew exactly what I would do. I am going to write letters to you and in those letters I am going*

to reveal my feelings. I don't care whether you like what I am writing or not. For me the most important thing at this very moment is letting you know that you are on my mind. Please don't blame me for writing those words to you, blame nature, yes blame nature that made you so beautiful. I am just a messenger who delivers the message to you. Even if you kill the messenger, the fact is undisputable: you are beautiful, you are lovely, and you are admirable. Unfortunately I can't sing, but if I could I would be singing Luis Armstrong song "What a Wonderful World". I can't sing but I am singing it anyway "I see trees of green, red roses too. I see them bloom for me and you. And I think to myself, what a wonderful world...Lalalalalalaaaaaaaa." I hope you can see what your beauty has done to me...

Dear young lady, please let me know whether I shall continue writing to you or whether you prefer me to stop it at this moment. Please write a reply and send the letter to 'vojin'Jirka, kasarne Hradec Kralove, Czech Republic.

Best regards,
Your admirer
Jirka

"Jirko, come here, read. Tell me what you think about this."

Jirka read the letter, smiled and said, "that is good. She would like that. I bet she would. Hmm…"

"What hmm, is there something that you don't like?" Jozef asked Jirka.

"Yeah," Jirka said, "the ending of the letter. What if she chooses not to continue?"

"Well, you would have to accept that!" Jozef said to Jirka.

"I don't like that." Jirka said.

Jozef was not sure whether Jirka sent the full version of a letter or whether he made some changes.

After a week Jirka came to Jozef with wide smile on his face.

"Jozef, look what I've got…" he said waving a white envelope.

"What is that?" Jozef kind of knew what he had, "a reply letter from your sweetheart?"

"Yes, it is," Jirka's round face was all sparkling, smile from one ear to another, "do you want to open it and read?"

"Jirko, the recipient address on the letter says your name, you should open and read it!"

"You wrote a letter to her, you should read it as well". So Jirka opened and read loudly:

> *Dear Jirko,*
> *I came home today and what a surprise: "a letter for me!"*
> *Who is this letter from? It is from Jirka! Jirko, we have met*
> *two times so far and you are writing a letter to me! It is so*
> *nice of you and your letter has been written so nicely. I wish*
> *you were next to me and could whisper to my ear the words*
> *that you wrote for me☺. I wish my mother would be nicer.*
> *She saw the letter and did not like that. She doesn't want me*
> *to date you! She is telling me that I am too young for you.*
> *Seventeen is not too young! I think she is against me dating*
> *any boy. She would say that each boy wants the same thing: to*
> *get a girl to the bed only. She tells me that I must be careful,*
> *that I must not trust you. I asked my mom whether is it OK*
> *if I kiss you only, nothing else. My mom allowed me only a*
> *very short kiss, lasting not longer than two seconds. Jirko, I*
> *can't wait until you get home from Hradec Kralove. I will*
> *give you a dozen two-second kisses☺.*
> *And yes, you can write to me again and please write as much*
> *as you can.*
> *Yours,*
> *Margareta*

Jirko stopped reading and looked at Jozef with a very happy face. Jozef was little bit envious (he wrote the letter and she replied to Jirka!) still at the same time Jozef was happy for Jirka.

"Jozef, what should I write now? You have to help me. I don't know what I should write?!"

"Jirko, you should write! I don't know the girl…" Jozef reacted.

5

"You have to help me; you wouldn't do that to me. You started, you have to continue…"

"OK, ok, what is your objective? What you would like to achieve?"

"What? I don't understand. You sound like a high school teacher. What are you talking about?"

"What is your plan? What you would like to do with Margareta?"

"I want her to come here, to Hradec Kralove, and I want to have sex with her…"

"Hahahahaah Jirko, don't be a red neck! Yes, you can say that to me but please don't write that to her. You have to play a game; otherwise you would just confirm what her mom said in the letter."

"Whose mom? Do you know her mom? What game are you talking about?" Jirka was confused.

"No, I don't know her mom. You just read the letter; didn't you notice that she mentioned her mom? And you are saying you don't know what game you need to play?"

"She wrote that she would kiss me…" again a wide smile on Jirko's face, "no, I don't know what game you talking about."

"Play a game, you know like you try to impress her, the game that every soul is playing when consciously or unconsciously that soul is revealing its attraction to its other half; the half that every soul is constantly searching for. The soul doesn't have to be just a human being. There are plenty examples from nature too. Have you ever observed a rooster and a hen? The rooster chooses a hen and runs after her; the hen runs too, but only for a few seconds. Then the hen stops, kneels down a little bit, the rooster hops on the hen and they mate." Jozef said earnestly, his big brown soulful eyes intense.

"Ha ha haa ha, that is funny, no I have never observed that…"

"There is also a game between lions. When a lion wants to mate, the male lion has to follow his chosen female lion for several weeks, if not months. I saw a movie on the National Geographic channel about their mating. Only after several weeks of a male lion following a female lion would that female lion let the male mate with her."

"Hahaha, is that so? The male lion follows the female for such a long time, he must be stupid. What if a male lion is following a female lion for several weeks or months, as you are saying, and she will still not let him mate? Isn't the rooster game a better option? And a rooster has lots of chickens that he can start chasing and he is rewarded after just several seconds of running. I want to play the rooster game!"

Jozef laughed loudly. "It's not only what you would like to play, you have to get the female who will agree to play that particular game. Hey, please don't tell Margareta: "Let's play rooster-hen game...""

They were both laughing now.

Jozef then added, "I didn't think about that awful option that a male lion might face. You know what I once did? I counted exactly how long the rooster-hen game takes. A rooster starts chasing a hen. A rooster might think *this is a nice chick I am going to get her* and starts running after that particular chick. A chick might think: *ha, you think you would get me so easily, no, no, no, run if you want something and you better run fast* and she starts running away. I am observing and counting: 21, 22, 23, 24, 25 the rooster catches the hen and he hops on her: 26, 27, 28, 29, 30 the rooster is done, jumps down from a hen, he stretches, his head is up, his wings spread out and a loud sound comes out of his throat: cock-a-doodle-doooooo.... So I am thinking the game is over, they play their game as it is written in their genes; what a nice reward I guess, why otherwise would a rooster would announce loudly his good feeling and why a hen, after finishing the mating extravagance, would be so happily continuing her daily routine."

"Ha ha ha, you are so funny. So their game lasted about 10 seconds only?" Jirka asked.

"Yeah, 10 seconds. I would say that since the lion's game is longer it might hide bigger fun. A lion has to follow a female lion carefully, so she will not refuse him and run away forever. I don't think that in the rooster-hen game that rooster would not ever catch his hen. I have never observed the lion's game in real life so I can't tell for sure. I would think it is probable that a male lion doesn't always get his female sweetheart. I guess if there is another male lion interested in that particular beautiful female lion, the male lion has to scare and chase his rival away from her, otherwise he would lose her. I guess when lions finally mate it takes much longer than the four seconds rooster gets for his mating. So what would be more enjoyable? Hahaha, you tell me..."

"Give me a break! I am not into that philosophy. So are you going to write something or not?"

"Give me a pen and piece of paper please…"

Jozef took a pen that Jirka had ready for him and started to write:

> *Dear Margareta,*
>
> *The sun was shining more brightly today and I know why. I received a letter from you. I was so happy to see that envelope. I read your letter several times and always felt happiness inside of me. Yes, a dozen two-second kisses are all I would like to get. I would enjoy each of them very much. I can imagine how your lips would taste. I think they would taste as chocolate-covered strawberries… I want to write also about something else. I think I know why I like to look into your eyes. I remember you asked me 'what?' when I looked into them. I should have replied that I see sky in your eyes and when I ask you "how do you do?" your answer with head lightly confirming your answer: "I am OK" made me puzzled…*

Jirka watched over Jozef's shoulders, his dark brown hair flopping over his forehead.

"What are you writing? I never told her "how do you do." I don't remember looking into her eyes. Chocolate-covered strawberries?? Ha ha ha… I have to laugh; can't you come up with something else?"

"Something else?! You write it if you are so smart! When I write I am writing to a real person, or better say, to a person that exists is my imagination."

"So you are saying that you are writing to somebody else? So you are not really writing to Margareta? To whom then are you writing? You are cheating!"

"I am saying that I have to imagine somebody real when I am writing and I have to feel that this particular person likes what I am writing. Yes, you might consider this as cheating. You can write your own ideas if you prefer! You asked me to write, so I am writing! You want to be truthful? Hahaha… '*The truth is a lie, but it has a hint in it*' read Levi's book that Julo has on his bed; that sentence is right there. You agree that there is hint in my writing and any girl might like that writing, not only my imaginary one. Have you heard what Nietzsche said about the truth? *The only truth is the lived truth!*"

"You are talking too much. Don't be so upset; write whatever you want to write so I can send it to Margareta..." Jirka mumbled under his breath.

So Jozef did. Jirka then sent the second letter to Margareta and they were both counting the days. Mail from Hradec Kralove to Prague takes about 2-3 days. So today was Monday. She should get this letter Thursday or Friday. If she wrote an answer the same or the next day then they should receive something from her by the end of next week.

Jirka couldn't wait for next week to come. He was really looking forward to getting a reply from Margareta. Whenever they had free time—usually later afternoon or in the evening—he wanted to talk to Jozef.

"Jozef, do you think she will reply? Do you think she will write something back? What if she finds another boy more attractive? Or if she simply would rather not bother to write an answer? Girls do that. Don't they? They have a boyfriend, a big love. Then he must go for this two-year stupid nonsense: 'serving your country' prison, and what does she do? She goes with the first boy that she meets at a disco-party. Do you think Margareta is different? Do you think that she will wait until I get back home?"

Jozef smiled at him.

"You are in love with her aren't you? Or are you just lonely and would like to communicate your feelings with somebody?"

"I don't know. Both? Have you been in love? To whom you are writing anyway? I see the pictures of two gorgeous girls on your desk. Who are they? Are you chasing two girls at the same time? Like that rooster? One is not enough?"

"You are getting smart very fast, aren't you?! One of them is my younger sister."

"Which one? Would you introduce me to her?"

No... I would keep her far away from you..."

Jozef would rather keep his personal stuff for himself. He never liked to share his inside feelings with anybody else. He didn't understand how people could loudly talk about their intimate relationships; talk about what they did, how they did it, with whom they did it, who else might be next. Jozef was in platonic love by the time he was 14. He would never tell anybody about his feelings. On the other hand, he wanted to be heard, to be heard by her and only by her and he would like it if she kept that feeling to herself as he did. But how to do that? How to accomplish all those objectives? Not an easy task for fourteen-year-old. The boiling inside of him was visible. No matter how he tried to hide his feelings, some girls could figure it out and without hesitation asked Jozef, "Are you dating Ann?"

"Not yet." Jozef replied automatically. *'Gosh what I have just said?'* Jozef would think… *That was a slip of my tongue! I want to take that back! I am not trying to start dating anybody! Can you hear that! They figured out my feeling towards her! I would like to start dating her, that is the truth, but I don't know how! And I definitely don't want anybody to know about that!* Jozef would love to spend time with Ann and Ann only. That would be the correct, honest answer. Jozef's unrequited love never converted into reality.

The reply letter from Margareta came as Jozef and Jirka were anticipating, the following Friday.

"Jozef, here it is! A letter from Prague! From Margareta! Come here, let's read it!"

Jozef didn't feel good about it. This should be Jirka's private, secret time. He should read the letter alone, for him only. *Not everybody is built the same way* Jozef thought… and Jozef was curious anyway and would like to know what was written there. Jozef wrote the letters and he wanted to know the answer.

The letter that Jirka received:

> *Dear Jirko,*
> *I should rather write my Jirko, Jirko, Jirko, Jirko… I like to pronounce your name. I like to do that loudly. I was in my room doing just that when my mom entered my room. She heard what I was saying. She didn't say anything, but I saw she was not happy. I mean she didn't said anything at the beginning, then she said something about condoms and not getting pregnant, and her voice got louder and louder and she almost started yelling at me! But I don't care. I started to write my daily journal. I am writing there about my feelings. Do you want to know what I am writing about? You would*

laugh at me. I will write that in my next letter if you want me to. How soon you will you come to Prague? I was wondering whether I should go to Hradec Kralove. My mom wouldn't like that idea. I know that for sure. I won't ask her. If I did decide to come I would not tell her anything, I would just go.
Do you want me to come to Hradec Kralove?
Sending you a million kisses,
Yours Margareta.

Jirka finished reading and looked at Jozef, with a 'what now?' expression on his face.

"What now Jozef? What we should do now? Should I go to Prague or should I ask her to come here?"

"What should *we* do? What should *we* do? What *you* should do? Margareta is your girl-friend, not mine! You do whatever you want to do!"

Don't be harsh to him! Josef thought to himself. *You are jealous! You are writing to two girls now (one of them Margareta, the second one your big love) and the incorrect one is replying the way you wish the other would!*

Jozef's inner monologue was disrupted by Jirka's voice, "Wait a minute! You wrote the letters! Why are you upset? Would you help me to write to her and ask her to come to Hradec Kralove, please?"

Jirka knows how to smile and beg nicely. Jozef felt bad. Felt bad about his thoughts, his jealousy.

"It would be so much easier if she could come here, don't you agree? You know how hard is to get a day or two off from this stupid place. And I really want to see her. I want to be with her."

"OK Jirko, I will write for you, something irresistible so she will come, I am positive she will. By the way, you want to be with her only, nothing else, right?"

"What do you mean? Of course I want to be with her."

"You remember the game we were talking about last time; have you forgotten?"

Jirka smiled, "No, I haven't forgotten. You mean the rooster-hen game? Don't you have something that is not as long as lion-game but would last little bit longer than the rooster-hen game? Hahaha... You know what?

I don't know – she might be a virgin. What if she is? What should I do then?"

Jozef didn't like this type of discussion. Discussions about girls that might be virgins. Boys would complain: *'Virgins don't know how they should do it and they might cry and it is not pleasant experience…'*brrr, Jozef preferred not to participate in this kind of discussion.

"No, I don't know what you should do. Let me rather write."

> *Dear Margareta,*
> *I had a dream last night. I spent all day with you. We were not talking at all. We were just together all day long. Whenever I looked at you, you were smiling. Your face bright, your smile so beautiful. You let me hold your hand and I was happy that I could do that; hold your hand, be next to you, look at you, no words, just holding your hands, looking into your eyes and then running, running hand in hand…*

"So romantic… how do these thoughts come to your mind?" Jirka is again watching over Jozef's khaki shoulders.

"What Jirko? You don't like it?"

"No, no, I like it. I am just wondering, how easily you write. Hey, and don't forget to ask her to come to Hradec Kralove and write her that she doesn't need to be worried about condoms, I will get some…"

Hm, write about condoms… Jozef thought, to buy a condom in the 80s was not so easy. A young man would have to go to the pharmacy store, go to the sales countertop and face a (usually) older, strict looking woman who would know him (as she did almost everybody in the small city).

"Good afternoon, can I have please a condom?" A boy (young man) would almost whisper in his uncertain voice.

"What? What do you want? Speak louder young man! I couldn't hear you and thus couldn't understand!" a woman at the sales countertop would reply to the boy's demand.

"Uhm, uhm" the young man would clear his throat and say little bit louder, "I would like to buy, uhm, uhm, a condom please…"

"What?" the woman would reply, now not because of boy's quiet speech but because of her surprise about the unexpected demand, "a condom? You want to purchase a condom?"

"Yes please…" the ashamed boy would reply, pay for the product and run away from the store. The number of condom sales would increase during Halloween season. The same boy would enter the store incognito, wearing a Halloween mask. By not revealing their identity the young man would be brave now and loudly announce entering to the store, "Good afternoon Mrs. Cerna, I would like to purchase 3 packs of condoms!"

Mrs. Cerna would look at a boy, say nothing and give the boy three packets of condoms.

"Well, do you have different brands Mrs. Cerna? I don't like this one. Which one you would recommend? Mrs. Cerna?"

"Recommend?" Mrs. Cerna's face would get little bit red.

"Yes, I would like to know which one is better. I heard that if you use a certain brand it gives you more pleasure! And frankly I don't have too many experiences. I thought you might be able to give me some advice Mrs. Cerna…. And by the way, which brand do you prefer to use Mrs. Cerna? Would that brand up there give you the higher pleasure or you would recommend some other…?"

"What about abstinence you small cheeky creature…"

In that moment the young fellow knew what he must do: run away, as fast as he can…

Jozef said to Jirka, "I am not going to write about any condoms. You write that if you want to… if you would like to be a butcher then do the butchering by yourself."

"What butcher? You are sometimes too strange. Give that letter to me. I am going to finish the writing."

Jirka then added his own writing:

Dear Margareta,
I had a dream last night. I spent all day with you. We were not talking at all. We were just together all day long. Whenever I looked at you, you were smiling. Your face bright, your smile so beautiful. You let me hold your hand. I was so happy that I could do that; hold your hand, be next to you,

look at you, no words, just holding your hands, looking into your eyes and then running, running hand in hand... Hey Margareta and don't worry about condoms, you know I have a friend, he is working as a helper in the pharmacy store, you know, I had a damn good chat with him, you know, we were drinking beer, having a good time, you know, I asked him about condoms and stuff like that, you know and he is going to bring three packets of condoms for me. I think, you know, that there are five or six condoms in each packet. So, you know, I was counting how many we would probably use in one night, you know and I am pretty much sure we should have enough of them, also for next time you come here to Hradec Kralove. You are coming here, right? You said that in your letter so I am already counting on that. And tell your mom she doesn't need to be worried about condoms and stuff like that and you know I was going to ask, do you have any experience in that stuff?, You know, sex and that kind of stuff? If not, don't worry I'll teach you, you know they are saying I am good at that, not teaching, in that stuff, you know what I mean. So come here as quickly as you can, let me know when so I can prepare all the stuff you know.

"Jirka, are you serious? Are you going to send her that letter?"

"Yes," Jirka answered with his typical smile. "Is there something wrong?"

"Well, yes, but you do what you would like to do." After short pause Jozef continued. "...and you are not going to comment on her daily journal?"

"What journal?"

"She wrote in her letter that she started to write her daily journal. You should let her know that you noticed that and perhaps write something nice about it. You could learn a lot about her from that journal. I guess she would be willing to share her writing with you."

"How do you know that? How do you know that she would share that stuff with me?"

"She asked in her letter whether you would like to know what she is writing. You read her letter just a minute ago. You should pay bigger attention to the words and their meaning when you are reading."

"Oh well. Too much talking. I want her to come here; you are making stuff much more complicated that it needs to be."

Jirka took the letter, didn't write anything else and sent it as he wrote it. Days went kind of slower after Jirka sent his version of the letter. Jirka and Jozef waited for the answer, waited and waited, no response. So they had to figure out what to do next…

Weeks in the *kasarne* sometimes went quite quickly; sometimes the time passed very slowly. Jozef was in charge of checking the radio equipment on five MiG-21 fighter aircrafts. The Russian made Mikyan-Gurevich MiG-21 supersonic jet aircraft were considered to be very good fighters at that time (first fly of MiG-21 was in 1955, in 1980 there were about 40 of them in Czechoslovakia). It was lightweight fighter and thus was good at maneuvering in the air. By the structure and performance MiG-21 was comparable to the American Lockheed F-104 and Northrop F-5 or to the French Dassault Mirage III. Jozef had to physically check every piece of communication equipment that was part of MiG-21. During his routine maintenance check-up he touched every antenna on the body of the aircraft to make sure that it was not loose. After he visually and physically checked equipment outside of the plane he sat in the aircraft's pilot seat and tested the communication with the airport control tower. He turned the knob to a certain frequency, pressed the knob and started talking.

"This is Second Lieutenant Jozef from Captain Mravec's maintenance group. Can you hear me? Switching over!"

"This is Second Lieutenant Svoboda at the control tower. I can hear you. Switching over!"

"Is that you, Vlada? I am in the MiG-21 number L354 doing regular maintenance check-up. Testing the connectivity to the control tower. Can you hear me clearly? Switching over!"

"Yes, Jozef. I can hear you clearly. Can you hear me clearly? Switching over!"

"Yes, Vlada. I can hear you clearly. This completes my radio testing. Switching over."

"Thanks, Jozef. See you."

Most of the time the maintenance check-up of all five aircrafts went quickly. When Jozef was done with the last aircraft he remained in the pilot's seat with the helmet on his head. He started to browse through radio frequencies until he heard in the built-in speakers of his helmet the public radio station 'Hviezda' (= star). There were not too many radio stations on which he could listen to music; Hviezda was one of them. He closed his eyes and listened to the music until the evening scheduled assembly of all units.

Jirka was in charge of the food supply. His assignment was to make sure that the food that supposed to be delivered was delivered and that when the food was delivered it wouldn't be stolen before it got to the kitchen for cooking. He didn't like to spend too much time in the food storage compartment. When he was done with his duties he rather went to the aircraft's parking area to spend time with Jozef or other the soldiers during their maintenance time. The parking space for each aircraft was a big turtle-back shape lying on the ground with big gates through which the aircraft could get in and out of the hangar.

"Jirka, can you see that dark spot above this MiG-21?" asked Jozef when Jirka came while he was checking antennas on one of the aircrafts.

"Yes; it's painted black. Why did they paint only that spot?"

"Come. I will show you something below the pilot's seat. Do you see that pull-out string below the seat?"

"Where, this one?"

"No, no, on the right side, under the seat. There is only one, see it?

"Ooo that one, this is for pilot's catapulting, right?"

"Yes it is. When Mravec showed us for first time how we do the maintenance he said several times 'Don't touch anything in the pilot's cabin that you are not supposed to touch' and then he pointed his finger to that spot on the ceiling and continued 'If you touch or pull what you shouldn't, you might end up like this poor guy Janosh. He got into the pilot's seat. He pulled the catapulting string. You wouldn't want to see what I saw.' And then he described the scene in detail…"

"You're kidding… he ejected himself from the aircraft here in this hangar? You think he did it on purpose or it was an accident?"

16

"I thought it was an accident. But now when you are asking… who knows… but I tell you if it was not an accident I wouldn't want to end my life like that!"

"Me neither and have you heard the story of what happened two years ago?"

"Which one do you mean?"

"The one about a guy who was hanging missiles under the wing."

"No I didn't. He was hanging real missiles?"

"No, fake ones, just for fly training purposes. But still the missile looked like a real one, was sharp on the front end. The guy outside was hanging the missile under the wing and the guy inside was playing with the string on left side and he pulled the missile release string right after guy outside finished hanging the missile; the missile was released got into guy's body just penetrating him; he was running with this missile inside of his body for awhile until he collapsed and then died."

"Ufff, that is not fun."

"You bet not; still you could hear laughing from some empty brains that saw him running and then described him running 'like a chicken without a head hahaha'…"

"Hmm, some people think that everything can be turned into humor."

On the third week after Jirka mailed his (and Jozef's) letter to Margareta, Jirka came to Jozef in their spartan room and said, "I have a bad feeling Jozef. Something happened. We are not getting any letters from Margareta."

"Why you are talking in plural? You, singular person, you, are not getting anything from Margareta. I bet her mom read the last letter and convinced her to stop any communication with you," Jozef responded to Jirka's complaints.

"Do you think so? I didn't write anything that should piss her off, did I?"

"Maybe not her, but surely her mom."

"Her mom? Why is she letting her mom read my letters?"

"Hahaha…your letters? Yes, sorry for being ironic, they are your letters… maybe her mother just sneaked into Margareta's room and checked her personal stuff. You know, she wants to protect her daughter…"

"Shoot, what should I do? I am going to jump the concrete fence Friday night, go to Prague and come back Sunday evening," he said resolutely, "Will you cover me during the time I am not here?"

"Jirko, you know what would happen if they find out that you are missing. You and I will go to army jail."

It happened that some soldiers had run away for the weekend. Each morning and evening all servicemen in a unit had to stand up in a line on the hallway. A supervising, higher ranking soldier would read the name of each serviceman. After a name of a soldier was read, the particular soldier was supposed to say 'here' to confirm his presence. If somebody were covering for the missing guy then that person would say 'here' when the name of the missing soldier was read. It was common practice. Some higher ranking, supervising soldiers didn't care whether somebody was missing or not. But most supervising soldiers were jerks and made life hell if they found that somebody was missing and somebody else was covering for him.

Jozef knew that Jirka didn't care about that. He would just run away and Jozef would have to cover for him.

"Jirka, let's wait one more week and if we don't get anything from Margareta then we will decide what to do," Jozef suggested. This proved to be good suggestion because the following Friday Jirka ran into their unit room and yelled, "Jozef, we got it! A letter is here!"

"Jirka, slow down. There might be something in that letter that you will not like very much," Jozef cautiously warned Jirka.

Jirka opened the letter and started to read:

> *Dear Jirko,*
> *I hope my mom won't find out that I am writing to you. When I received your last letter I read it and put the letter on my desk. My mom saw your letter and read it. She then told me that you must be a schizophrenic person and should see a shrink. I didn't know what schizophrenic means. When I asked my mom what schizophrenic means she again raised her voice and said that she had warned me from the beginning about you. That I shouldn't be mislead by your earlier letters. She pointed to the second half of your last letter and told me that it looks to her that you have some*

kind of bipolar personality disorder problem and that you might be even an alcoholic. I re-read your letters and I thought to myself that my mom might be correct. The way you wrote the beginning of your last letter is different to the end. I can see why mom is saying that you have bipolar personality or even schizophrenia. I was then thinking about that over and over again. I found an article about schizophrenia and got scared. The symptoms described in the article include delusions, disordered thoughts and speech, and even hallucinations. Then I thought about how I saw you twice, but I didn't notice any of those symptoms. Is my mom over-reacting? She probably got angry because of your sentence about condoms. I can understand that; she is an older generation. I don't know whether condoms existed when she was young. She got pregnant with me after she had her first date with my father and got married very young. She doesn't want me to end up the same way. She reminds me of that over and over again. When she starts telling me her story, again, I have to tell her "Mom stop. I got it! I know what happened when you had your first date." Jirko, would you go and talk to a shrink? They must have a shrink in the army, don't they? I want to be sure that there is nothing wrong with you. I don't want to lose you. The army shrink would confirm that you are OK, wouldn't he? I can then tell my mom that she was overreacting and that you are not really crazy.
Yours, Margareta

A burst of laughter erupted after Jirka finished reading Margareta's letter.

"She is smart, Jirko. When she reads, she pays attention to what is written. You should learn that from her."

"She wants me to see a shrink!? Can you imagine? Going to a shrink office? Hello doctor Shrink. My girlfriend is not sure whether I am cuckoo or not. Can you just please sign a diagnosis confirming that I am a very normal person?"

"Are you? Are we? Ha ha ha… I am not so sure. Jirko, a shrink would more than likely also give you some IQ tests."

"IQ test? What is that?"

"You don't know what an IQ test is? Intelligenz-Quotient, a German term originally coined by psychologist William Stern. You take several quizzes, for example put in order some triangles, squares, circles, put in order numbers, solve some puzzles etc. You would then receive a score. I am guessing your score would be 50+"

"Is that good?" Jirka smiled with enquiring eyes.

"For a mentally retarded person, yes, quite good… Jirko, I am joking! No please don't hit me! I am joking…" Jozef was not sure whether Jirko was hurt by his comment and really was going to use his muscle advantage against Jozef's much smaller body.

"OK, seriously. I would say if your score is between 80-110 points in an IQ test you could consider yourself a person with average IQ. Albert Einstein got 160, Pascal and Baruch Spinoza around 170, Michelangelo, Da Vinci and Newton got around 190, which I think is the highest score."

"Have you ever taken the test? What is yours? Below 30?" Jirka asked Jozef.

"Yep, 30 might be good guess. I have taken so many tests in my life but the IQ. I would not beat you in IQ test Jirko though, that is a sure thing…" Jozef smiled at Jirka. Jirka liked Jozef's assumption.

"I read somewhere that Baruch Spinoza was the most intelligent person who ever walked on the Earth. He still doesn't have the highest score. I would guess the IQ test is not the exclusive indicator of human intelligence."

"Who was Spinoza? I have never heard this name."

"Let's talk about that some other time. I've got an idea what we should write back to Margareta. Sorry, Jirka. Am I stepping on your toes? You didn't ask me to write. You probably want to reply to her letter, don't you?"

"Ha ha…" with typical Jirko smile, "right, Jozef, please would you write what you think would be the best answer."

Jozef wrote:

Dear Margareta,
I was waiting anxiously for your letter and relieved when
it was finally delivered to my hands. I am sorry that my
last letter caused you so much trouble. I re-read that letter.

(You might wonder how I could re-read a letter that is now sitting on your desk. No, no I am not magician. I sometimes write using carbon-paper to retain copies of my writing.) I re-read that letter and must say that I understand why it could make an impression that there is something wrong with the author of that letter. I was thinking about your suggestion of going to a shrink. First I refused that idea on the spot but then slowly I changed my mind and decided to please you. I have a good friend here in the kasarne. He is not exactly a shrink but he likes to do soul analysis and he believes he could do as good an exam as a professional shrink would do. And he did. He looked at me; he physically checked all the important points of my body, as a doctor would do. He asked me to show him my tongue, he looked in my ears, my eyes, and he listened to my heart. He even hit my bended knee, to test my reflexes (at least he said so). Then he started to ask me such strange questions: whether my parents are divorced, whether I had any horrible events in my childhood and so on. I answered all his questions honestly and then he told me that his diagnosis is: love. He said that I must be in love. I don't know how he could come up with such an answer, but he did. He also told me that the woman with whom I am in love must possess tremendous power. He said that not all women have this gift. He said that you possess that kind of power though. You might not even know that this power is inside of you. He said that this type of power can trigger in a man such things as writing poems, writing books, creating unforgettable movies or in science making the biggest discoveries. I asked him about schizophrenia and that bipolar personality stuff. I have heard those words but I am not sure of their meaning. He confirmed that I am not schizophrenic, nor do I have a bipolar personality. Again, he is not a professional shrink but I think he knows what he is talking about. How do I know? I just know.

I was thinking about meeting you and talking to you in person. Unfortunately, I can't come to Prague. Not now. Believe me, if I could I would be next to you in a second. I would beat the speed of light. You are thinking that it is impossible to run as fast as light? I would at least try. Are you still planning to come to Hradec Kralove? If so, let me know when so I could arrange my time off.
Sincerely,
Jirka

"Good, good. This time I am not going to add anything else," said Jirka and he mailed the letter to Margareta.

Time passes slowly for someone who is waiting for a thing or event that is very important to him. Jirka wanted to kill that time and was not sure how. Jozef met him in the army sports-yard one afternoon.

Jirka surprised Jozef with a question, "Jozef, I was thinking about that IQ test. Can you tell me more about it?"

"What you want to hear?"

"I don't know. Do you have some examples that could be on that test?"

"As I said, I have never taken an IQ test. I liked logic puzzles though," Jozef said as he breathed more heavily as they jogged around the yard.

"OK, Jirko. Here is a question that you could get on the IQ quiz: You are in a train that is running at a speed of 150 miles per hour. You are a detective chasing Jack the Ripper. Both of you are in the same train. Jack the Ripper is in the first wagon, you are in the last. The train is in a curve. You look from the window and see Jack the Ripper's head in the window of the first wagon, he is trying to get out of the window. You pull your pistol and you shoot at Jack. The bullet from your pistol travels at a speed of 145 miles per hours. Will the bullet reach Jack the Ripper or not?"

"Not," Jirka answered with his typical smiley face.

"Why not?"

"The train runs 150 mph; the bullet is 5 mph slower, so it would never catch Jack the Ripper."

"OK, let's say now there is a second detective, Creye, watching the train from a grass field. He has exactly the same pistol as you do. He saw

Jack the Ripper as you did and shot from his pistol at Jack as well. Would his bullet reach Jack?"

"No, it would not," said Jirko.

"OK, what is the difference between the speed of your bullet from your pistol and the speed of the second bullet from a detective outside on the grass field?"

"I don't know. You tell me. What is the difference?"

"Jirko, think! You have two different systems, two frameworks. One system is the running train. You and Jack are part of that system. Your bullet shooting from your pistol is part of that system. Then you have second system: the grass field. The second detective, Creye, is part of that system. The puzzle is best solved from Creye's point of view. Creye sees the train running at the speed of 150mph. His bullet would never reach Jack the Ripper since the speed of his bullet is 5 miles slower, measuring both train speed and Creyes' bullet speed from the grass field. Now Creye looks at the train, the bullet speed is again measured from the grass field; the speed 150mph plus 145mph, thus your bullet will catch Jack the Ripper!"

"Hmm interesting. Who would say so? I think you are correct though."

"It is Einstein's theory of relativity for moving objects. Imagine that there is a closed system that is moving with steady speed such as the Milk Way Galaxy or our Solar System. If you are inside that moving system you would not be able to figure out if you are moving or not, or what the speed of that moving system is. You would have to do that outside of that system. You have to be outside to figure out that if you are inside the system that system is moving relative to the other system."

"Is that so? Even more interesting. How do you know?"

"I told you, it is not me. It was Einstein that figured this out. Looking at the world with the eyes of relativity. Imagine if you get into a spacecraft and that spacecraft could travel with the speed of light—which is the absolute highest possible speed—a little bit less than 300,000,000 meters per second, then you would not age. You would be forever as old as you are now."

"Cool. Is it possible to build that kind of spacecraft?"

"Not now. But who knows, maybe in the future it will be."

"Hm, that stuff is good Jozef, you got me. I like your physics."

Chapter 3: 59 passing moments of Julo's life (1961-2009)

"Safe Haven", the movie directed by Lasse Hallstrom, is an adaptation of Nicholas Spark's novel of the same name. The movie is about a young, married woman, Erin, who escapes from an abusive husband and arrives in a small town where she meets a widowed young, handsome father, Alex, with two small children. Alex's wife died a couple years ago from cancer. Alex and Erin start a romantic relationship. Erin's abusive husband, a policeman, finds her. Erin's husband is so bad that he deserves to be killed and he is. At the end of the movie story Alex gives a letter to Erin, which was written by Alex's wife. She knew she would die and wrote letters to the future: to their kids and to the future wife of her husband, who she knew he would eventually meet. Tears flow from the viewer of the movie when he listens to what she wrote to Julianne. The end of the Hollywood movie. The TV is then turned off...

One portion of Julo's life and *"Safe Haven"* was similar. Julo had been married for while; had two kids, then his wife died, of cancer too. As in the movie, he was a handsome, widowed man with two small children. After his wife died, when he was 48, he got married again. It was a big wish that his story would turn into the *"Safe Haven"* story; but it was not meant to be. On hearing how he ended his life, tears of joy are replaced by goose-bumps.

His last evening on the earth went like this: after dinner he opened the window in the kitchen of his 5th floor apartment, the window right above the kitchen chair. His kids were already in the bed. He came close to them, gave them each a kiss. Then he went to his wife, gave her a hug from behind. Then he ran towards the opened kitchen window... and jumped...

Why? Why did he jump? Julo loved his life, well, sure he loved it when he was kid; what kid doesn't love life?

<u>Passing moments 1 (1963-1968).</u>

Julo remembered when he became aware of himself; his brain got to the stage when back-linkage for self-awareness clicked in ... *'what is that? Me? Amazing, I am aware of myself'*. He was maybe 2 or 2 $^{1/2}$ years old? He remembered lots of things from his childhood. He remembered which girls he liked when he was seven; first it was Kathy, dark hair, sweet smile; Mary, blond hair, sweet smile; Vera, curly hair, sweet smile.

He remembered his thoughts before he fell asleep: he would grow up, he would have a nice car, he would walk next to his car and Kathy would smile at him, he would take her into the car for a ride, he would take Mary and Vera too; not all of them at once, he wouldn't do that, he would take them separately, he would enjoy that more than if he was to take them all together. He couldn't wait to be grown up; he was looking forward to being grown up and he happily fell into deep sleep each night.

He remembered how he observed the things surrounding him. Interestingly, some nights before he fell asleep he could hear sounds: bum, bum, bum... a rhythmic, regular sound; he heard the sound sometimes when his father was not home. On one particular evening he was convinced that the sound had been generated somehow to inform him that his father was not home. Only later, when he started going to school, did he realize how silly his thoughts were; the sound was generated by his heartbeat and he heard that sound because of the way he put his ear on the pillow.

He almost forgot how he hid under a bed one night when his father came home. Julo was about three years old and playing in the master bedroom. His dad came home and angrily yelled something at his mom; mom was crying, dad yelling "give me money, I need money! I earned it! I'll do with it whatever I want to..." They were both heading to the bedroom where mom had the family safe with money. Julo quickly crawled under the bed before mom and dad entered the bedroom. Dad's loud, angry yelling and mom's heartbreaking crying continued for a while; neither of them knew that their little son was under the bed. Julo didn't understand that his dad was drunk and wanted to get money to go back to the pub to continue drinking there. He hide away by instinct, he didn't even notice that his body was shivering. At that time he didn't know that what he felt under that bed has a name: fear.

Passing moments 2 (1968-1969).

Julo couldn't wait to go to school. The elementary school was in the same building as the middle school. The middle school students had classes in the morning 8am-12:30pm, elementary school children 1-5pm. The afternoon children usually waited at the school entrance before the school doors were opened for them to enter the building around 2:45pm. Julo walked to school by himself. Most first grade kids walked to school; even it took 30 minutes or so. Julo usually got to the school building around 12:30pm and waited with other kids to enter the school.

One day when Julo got to the school building he didn't see any children waiting at the front. He didn't know what he should do. Their first grade elementary school teacher was a strict person. She told them that everybody must be on time and be sitting in their chairs by 12:55pm so when she entered the classroom at 1:00pm everybody was there. He got scared. He already knew how adults could throw their anger, that it didn't matter who the recipient of their mood was, it didn't matter who caused their boiling anger. He was afraid he would have to face something similar from the teacher. He didn't see anybody at the front of the school, he would rather not go in, so he turned back and went home.

"Why you didn't go in?" asked his mother, "the class hadn't started yet. Yes, nobody was at the front of the building because the school door was opened a couple of minutes earlier. You still had enough time to sit at your chair before teacher came in, and even if not; you don't have to be afraid if you come little bit later, it's no big deal."

It was not a big deal for his mom, but it was for Julo; he wanted to be on time. He measured the time by the group of kids at the front of the school, and the kids were not there which meant he was late. He didn't want to face the teacher's reaction to him being late, he'd rather not go in. It was then that he realized that time should not be measured by events only; he'd seen those nice hand watches and he now understood better their purpose; he couldn't wait until he got his own watch, the same as older kids had on their wrist.

Passing moments 3 (1970).

"Julo, have you seen a dead body?" asked Stanley, a cousin one year older.

"A dead human body? No I haven't" Julo knew why his cousin was asking him about a dead body. There was a huge car accident over the weekend; two teenagers dead, three young adults survived with heavy injuries. Among the dead was a fourteen-year-old girl from their neighborhood: Gitka Krskova. Her dead body, which had been lying in the open coffin, could now be viewed in the living room in the house where Gitka use to live. Julo heard from several kids who had the courage to go there and look at dead Gitka how scared they were before they entered the room. They described how everybody who was there in the room was crying, how older women were sitting next to the coffin and were loudly repeating prayers.

"So come with me to see Gitka. I was there already with Tony".

"You were there with your brother Tony? He is much older than you are so it was easier not to be scared to go there."

"Ha, I would go there even by myself. It's nothing. I am not scared. Come with me."

Julo was hesitating but the curiosity won. He slowly followed Stanley to Krskova's house. They entered the living room, the window curtains made the room dark even during the mid of the day. The toll candles on the back of the coffin were lightening Gitka's yellow face; face completely different than Julo remembered from the middle school hallways. Gitka was a girl with dark, curly hair and often-a-little-bit red cheeks on an otherwise snowy white face. How this could be? The dead body belongs to Gitka, Julo knew that, but her face had changed so much. Julo could hear the repeated praying of six women sitting close to the side wall: "Our Father, who art in heaven, hallowed be thy name, thy kingdom come, they will be done on earth as it is in heaven. Give us this day our daily bread and forgive us our trespasses as we forgive those who trespass against us and lead us not into temptation…"

Julo and Stanley were near window when they heard crying behind the door which was getting louder. It was Gitka's father who entered the room with loud crying: "Gitka mine, Gitka mine, please wake-up, please wake-up…" his tears were running down on his face when he came close to the coffin, he put his palms around Gitka's face, bent his body and started to kiss Gitka's face: "Gitka, mine Gitka wake-up! Wake-up please…" He put his cheek on Gitka's yellow cheek and whispered to Gitka's ear with softly-crying voice "wake-up, Gitka, wake-up"… Two other men entered the room. Julo didn't know them, they were Mr. Krstka's relatives.

"Anthony, come, you can't stay here, your heart will break completely, come with us outside."

"No, I want to be here. I want to be here with Gitka…. Gitka, wake-up." His tears were broken, he was broken. He then leaned on both men and walked out of the room. Six women were praying a little less loudly: "Holy Mary, Mother of God, pray for us sinners, now, and at the hour of our death…"

Passing moments 4 (1971).

Julo had good logic and he learned quickly and easily. Jan, his neighbor, taught him to play chess when Julo was eight and Jan was ten. Within two months Jan would rather not play chess; Jan couldn't win a chess game against Julo anymore.

Julo loved to be with his father. His father was not a heavy drinker; however when he got drunk he smelled badly and talked nonsense.

"You know, Julo, I didn't go to university because I couldn't but you must! Are you listening to me? You must! No other way around it…"

Why was daddy talking like that? What is going to university anyway, Julo thought.

Julo's father liked to spend his free time at their small farm and Julo loved to be around him during that time. He admired his daddy's skills; how his father built a shed or hen-house; how he took care of small pets, and they had lot of them.

Passing moments 5 (1972).

Julo's mom made him to go to church. Julo liked to go there but not all the time, not every Sunday morning as his mom would like him to. Julo was amazed by the huge church building; he was hypnotized by all the pictures on the walls, on the ceiling and on the glass windows. He was hypnotized by the statues and sculptures of the saints: something to admire. He absorbed each word that Father Komornik said during mass.

One evening mom insisted he had to go to mass; it was big holiday. Julo didn't want to go because he had the hiccups. He couldn't control it. He tried to hold his breath as his friends recommended him to do; still the hiccups were there. He went to the church and sat in the front row with other small boys as he usually did. The mass started but the hiccups didn't.

In the middle of the mass Father Komornik took a wafer into his hands, and raised his hands while saying,

"And he took bread, gave thanks and broke it, and gave it to them saying, *this is my body given for you; do this in remembrance of me.*"

When Father Komornik finished this longer sentence there was a period of silence in the church during which everybody's eyes looked at Father Komornik's hands. The silence was suddenly broken by "Hic…hic…hic" Ooo gosh, now everybody is looking at Julo, even Father Komornik took his eyes off the wafer that was above his head in his straight arms. The father's eyes searched for the source of the disruption to the holy silence; it took him a tenth of a second before his eyes rested on Julo's guilty look. Poor Julo couldn't do anything but "Hic… hic…hic."

Passing moments 6 (1972).

Some readings repeated at each Sunday morning mass remained in Julo's memory for a long, long time.

"*Peace I leave with you; my peace I give you. I do not give to you as the world gives. Do not let your hearts be troubled and do not be afraid.*"

What Julo had a problem comprehending was the claim that God was everywhere, God could see everything and he could hear everything. How this could be? He didn't challenge Father Komornik's claim, but he was not convinced that this could be the case.

At the end of each month everybody attending church was supposed to attend confession as well. Julo's mom insisted that Julo do so too. Father Komornik (or some other visiting priest) would sit on a chair to one side of the confession station, and the person confessing would kneel on the other side and speak into the priest's ear. There was usually a line formed by people waiting to confess to the priest. Julo noticed that usually older people talked to the priest much longer than the younger ones or kids.

"Mom, why do older people speak to the priest much longer that everybody else does? Is it because older people have committed more sins?"

"Some of them have," she nodded, "and some of them are just telling Father Komornik all the stuff that is bothering them."

"So this is why they sit there so long, and I have to wait in the line, just so they can tell all their stories to the priest? Why they do that?"

Instead of answering Julo's question, his mom just repeated what Julo heard every Sunday at mass: "Lord, I am not worthy to have you come under my roof. But, just say the word and my soul will be healed."

Passing moments 7 (1973).

When Julo was in sixth grade his math teacher noticed Julo's talent.

During one class he surprised everyone, "I will be absent next week. We should start a new chapter, equation formulas with two unknowns. Julo, can you please do the presentation while I am not here? In your presentation you will explain to everybody how formulas with two unknowns can be solved, then do a few examples together with all the class. If something is not understood, please take notes and we will discuss that when I am back. Julo, please do not rush when you make your presentation. You like to go too fast with your thoughts. Slow down, and make your case so everybody in the room will understand what you would like to say or explain." The math teacher was serious.

Julo took this task seriously too. Once home he opened the math book, found the chapter about formulas with two unknowns. He knew that he had to understand how to solve the equation if he wanted to explain to anybody else how to approach working on the tasks. And he did. He learned quickly how to solve the equation formulas and prepared himself for the lesson.

The schedule of the math teacher changed however – he didn't go away as he said he would. He still let Julo be a teacher and asked him go ahead with his presentation. Julo stood up at the front of the class and started to explain how the formulas with two unknowns could be resolved. Then his tongue went dry; he controlled himself and tried to speak slowly. When the class ended he was exhausted. He liked the way he handled this task and so did his teacher. He later heard that the teacher had praised his performance in front of all the parents during the quarterly parents/teacher meeting.

Passing moments 8 (1973).

Julo didn't like Thursdays or Sunday afternoons. He didn't like Thursday because they had two classes that he didn't like at all: singing and painting. How he wished those classes would not exist. Sunday evening he didn't like because the two weekend days were coming to an end and the school week was just around the corner. He noticed that some Sunday nights before he fell asleep strange thoughts would come to his mind. He thought about who would be most sad if he died, who would cry most and who would like him to live rather than die. They were strange *'gloomy kind of bun'*, bitter-sweet thoughts. Perhaps it could be that those thoughts are written in DNA.

Julo would like to know what happened when people died. He and the other kids discussed this topic during their play-time gatherings quite often. Most kids claimed what they heard their parents say: if you are good person your soul will go to heaven; if you are bad your soul might end up in hell. From there, you could still get to heaven but you would have to go through a hard process of soul cleaning. Julo would like to go to heaven but he doubted that Saint Peter would let him go directly to heaven; he thought he would have to go through the soul cleaning process. He wanted to know how it felt when someone died. Was it the same as when his conscious mind turned into sleep? *If I could catch the moment when I go to sleep I could get into the stage of sleepiness and see what is like to be there,* he thought. He decided to try to catch the moment when his state of consciousness turned to unconsciousness; when his brain switches to deep sleep. For several nights in a row he tirelessly tried to control exactly when this switch happened, and monitored his thoughts and the stage of consciousness. He just couldn't grasp that particular millisecond when one stage turns into another.

Passing moments 9 (1973).

Julo loved to sit on the window trim inside the master bedroom and watch the neighboring property; it was for sale. A middle-aged couple with two kids bought the property and started to build a house. Julo was hypnotized by watching big machinery push the uneven ground away; different types of bulldozer pulled the ground to make space for the foundations.

He would watch the work going on at that property for hours and hours. During the weekends the bulldozers and big machinery were usually quiet and only the couple that bought the property were there. Julo watched them through the window. Even if window was closed he could hear their loud communication. It is not a regular type of communication; they often shouted at each other. Julo didn't understand what they were talking about, but he could see the rage on their faces.

"The couple that bought the property next door are strange people," said a neighbor to his mom as Julo stood quietly behind the stove in their living room listening, "they live in an apartment far away, in Kosice, and bought the property here to build a house. They think that moving from a big city to a smaller one will save their marriage. They have two small boys, Marko and Mathias. My sister lives in Kosice in same apartment building as they do. She told me everything about them," the neighbor with the quiet voice and wavy brown hair paused for breath before continuing with wide eyes, "he has some kind of strange brain illness. His father had the same illness and he inherited it. People with this disease live a normal life until a certain age. When they are about 50 years old this illness starts showing up and then they die shortly after that. The name of the disease is very strange. I can't remember it. Oh, yes, I remember now, it is schoziforia. It's very rare disease, it affects the brain and doctors do not know how to treat that sickness."

Julo breathlessly listened to the quiet, almost whispering voice of the neighbor from across the street. He liked to listen to her when she came to have a chat with his mom. When she came Julo would leave all his toys, and quietly hide behind the stove and focus all his attention on her stories.

Passing moments 10 (1974).

Julo's father was a veterinarian. He worked for a co-operative farm. The Czechoslovakian communist regime would not allow a private practice. Still, people helped each other without having an official private firm.

Being a vet in a village meant that people would knock at the door usually later in the afternoon, or over the weekend, and ask for help or advice if their domestic animals were sick.

"Daddy, Mr. Vranka is standing at the front door. He is asking whether you are home," said Julo.

"What the hell does he want? Again! And why did you tell him I am home!" blasted Julo's father with anger. Julo knew that his dad didn't like visitors, especially if they came right after he came home from work. When visitors came at that time he got very angry and threw his anger at whoever brought him the news about the visitor. This time it was Julo.

Even though he was angry he went to greet the visitor. His behavior changed 180 degrees. He could perfectly mask his anger.

"Hi Janko," Julo's daddy said with a broad smile on his face, greeting Mr. Vranka just a couple of seconds after his anger landed on Julo's soul. He greeted Mr. Vranka as if he was the most welcome guest coming to their house; as if he didn't have any anger inside of him. "How can I help you, Janko? Yes, yes, no problem..."

Julo could hear his father words. *Did Mr. Vranka know that he was not welcome?* Julo speculated. He knew that his father didn't want to be bothered when he was home and he knew daddy displayed his feelings one way to people within family and another way to people outside of the family. His father could perfectly mask his true feelings and could play pleasant host who welcomed a visitor to his house.

Passing moments 11 (1974).

Julo was in platonic love with Ella throughout all his middle-school years and the first two years of high school. Ella was one year younger than he was. His heart started to beat faster when he was near her, often during class breaks when all kids from each class had to go out for a short 10-minute walk. When their eyes met Ella would smile at him and he would smile at her.

Ella lived on the third floor of a seven-floor apartment building and Julo knew which window belonged to Ella's room. He knew it even though he had never been inside the apartment and he always looked at the window when he was walking by their apartment building. He wondered what Ella was doing at that moment; how he wished he could be a fly on the wall in Ella's room just to watch her. Julo never openly exposed his feelings to Ella and he wasn't sure whether she had any towards him. He started to write love poems, which he never gave to Ella.

Passing moments 12 (1974).

During his middle-school time Julo joined a group of boys his age that put together several soccer teams. They created their own soccer league and played once or twice a week. Julo was a goalkeeper. He enjoyed each game very much; he loved to catch the ball on penalty kicks. After each game they talked about who did what and what could be done differently. During that time period a new guy moved to their town from a rural area and joined their soccer group; his name was Jaro. Julo's friends made fun of Jaro.

"You should have seen Jaro, how happy he was when he saw a train for the first time in his life. He was running and yelling *train, train, ohhh I see train...*" Julo's friends laughed.

Julo thought to himself, *I don't understand why they are laughing. I would be as happy as Jaro is if I saw an airplane flying in the sky...* And he looked again at the sky, as he often did, closely examining the tremendous space above him. Nothing, no airplane, but the beautiful, blue sky.

Passing moments 13 (1975-1978).

The parents of teenagers learnt that Julo had a talent for explaining math to his fellow high school students, so they came to him and asked whether he could give extra math lessons to their sons or daughters. Julo was flattered to be approached by adults.

"No, I don't want anything for my extra math classes," was Julo's typical answer to how much he would charge for his lessons. He didn't refuse small gifts and was glad when he heard that his students improved in math after their extra lessons ended. Julo's dad was proud of his son's gifted talent. The way he expressed it, though, was awful; usually when he was drunk.

One afternoon he had few drinks after he left his work. On the way home he saw a group of young kids: Julo's friends. He stopped and started talking about Julo's talent.

"Guys, you know my son, right? He is so good in math; when he asked you math questions you would start to pee ink…" The kids laughed, and of course they told the story to Julo the next day. Julo was embarrassed. He could imagine his drunken father talking to his friends and didn't like that image at all.

A much stronger punch came several months later. Julo's father asked him whether he wouldn't mind giving math lessons to three adults, friends of his fellow coworker. They were planning to take the entry exam to college and needed help with refreshing their math knowledge. All three guys were already married, had their own kids. They needed to have a college degree in order to keep their current work position. Julo agreed. He held the lessons for two hours every Sunday for about three months.

Dad usually took Julo in his car to one of the fellow's houses on Sundays, and one Sunday they didn't go as Julo thought they were supposed to.

"They don't need math lessons anymore," was dad's answer when Julo asked. Three or four months later, Julo learned the real reason. His father got drunk at a party attended by all three of Julo's students. He told them that they were stupid and the way to get out of their stupidity was to take math classes given by his son. Julo could picture the scene at the party: "… wait a minute… wait a minute," his daddy would say, as he usually said when he was drunk "… I am going to tell you something… you know my son, Julo, he is especially talented… and I tell you something, you guys, you are stupid, not everyone can be intelligent, I am, you are not, you are stupid… you are stupiiid and my son had to give you math lessons, so there could be a way to get out of your stupidity…"

Why did he do that? Julo thought, *he embarrassed me, and himself, so much.* Julo was ashamed of his father's behavior. He didn't have the courage to say anything to his father; he was afraid to approach him. The fear of his father's anger was deeply seeded in Julo's brain. He knew how his father would react; he would get angry, he would not admit that he had done anything wrong. One thing Julo knew; he would never, never get drunk the way his father had done.

Passing moments 14 (1979).

When Julo turned 18 he started to work on getting his driver's license.

"Don't you think that you will be driving my car when you get your driving license!" his daddy's angry voice announced to him one Saturday morning when was leaving for a driving lesson.

Julo was not sure whether this had anything to do with the girl that he was seeing more often now. The girl's name was Lea and she was two years younger. She went to the same high school as Julo did, as a sophomore. She had sparkling eyes, curly hair, and a flirty smile. Her parents were divorced. Was that the reason she needed someone who would love her? Lea had chosen Julo for this task. It was not calculated pick; she needed someone and Julo crossed her path. It was Julo who put a small piece of paper with short poem into Lea's coat pocket that was hanging unattended in the dressing room. Julo didn't sign the paper but Lea knew it was him.

"Hello stranger, do you do that often?" Lea asked Julo one day as they stood by their lockers.

"Often what?" asked Julo.

"Write poems, put them in a girl's pocket and then play incognito?"

"No. That was my first time," he replied earnestly.

"It was nice poem. Are you going to write another one for me?" asked Lea.

"Would you read them?"

"I would love to…" a sweet smile accompanied the sparks in Lea's eyes.

So each night before Julo went to the bed he let his feelings be translated into poems, which he then gave Lea to read. Later a poem was accompanied by a rose. Julo didn't buy the roses from the store; he would not know where to buy them anyway. He first took a few roses from her mom's garden. Her mom would notice if he continued taking roses from her garden, so Julo started taking roses from the cemetery on the way to Lea's hose. He apologized to the gravestone: *"sorry. I know I should not do that. I know you don't mind though. I would not…"*

Julo lacked some of the social manners when giving Lea roses.

"Julo, when you give me something, look into my eyes, here," Lea would say to Julo with a smile while her two fingers pointed to her eyes. Lea wanted him to be with her when he is near her. Julo told her almost all his thoughts; she told him hers. Lea liked to dance so she convinced Julo to join her. They took dance lessons and participated in a dance competition; they had fun doing that. Time flew fast when they were together.

After six or seven months Julo realized that he was missing what he liked to do before he started dating Lea; he missed being himself. So he decided to cut off the relationship with Lea. He didn't realize that as Lea had started the relationship that he was not the one who was eligible to terminate it. After he announced his decision to Lea, within three days he received heartbreaking letter from her: *"... everybody who was close to me is leaving me... and I see that I am by myself on the dance floor..."* He couldn't sleep that night. She wanted him back; he couldn't let her suffer...

Within a week they were back together. Julo continued to write short poems to Lea; she continued to enjoy reading them. Lea loved receiving small presents, Julo loved to add them from time to time to a rose that he brought to Lea.

"Julo, my mom said that you are good at giving extra math lessons," said Lea one afternoon when they were walking together from school. Lea was not strong in math. So it was that during second year of his first dating experience he gave math lessons to his girlfriend.

Both Julo and Lea were virgins. Lea laughingly said that this was not a good combination; better if one of them had experience in that area. Julo didn't like this theory, nor did he like Lea saying it. Lea knew exactly how that extraordinary moment of her life should be. It would have to be in a special place, the room would be extraordinarily beautiful, with special lighting. Behind the open window would be the hum of nature, it would not have to be ocean. There would be a special song playing on the gramophone and this song would belong only to the two of them. She expressed her dream of it all to Julo and would not want to do it otherwise.

Julo remembered this and wanted to fulfill these imaginings. Lea's habit of postponing that moment by saying *'no, not now'* didn't bother him. He read in a teen magazine discussing the *'right time for it to happen'* that boys needed to learn to be patient, the right time would come. He decided to be patient.

37

Passing moments 15 (1979-1980).

Julo finished high school and then was accepted to study physics at University of Kosice. He moved out of his parent's house to live in the dormitory; a new chapter of his life began. The special kind of freedom— no parents' eyes— was something new for him and he enjoyed it. He looked forward to going home for the weekend though, mainly because he could be with Lea. The way they spent their time together changed now; since they didn't see each other every day as they used to, they both enjoyed time together more. Julo's mom didn't like it though; she wanted Julo to be home during weekends.

"Julo, do you think there will be no other girls when you are older? Believe me, this one won't be the only one in your life..."

Julo liked the guys with whom he shared his dorm room. He knew they liked each other as well. They decided to spend all five years of their graduate study together. They took most of the same classes and lived together throughout their student life. They knew how to enjoy the university life, how to spend time together, how to have fun together. They went to disco parties, and shared their thoughts about life's issue, such as faithfulness to their girlfriends. Julo didn't think much about faithfulness. It was something that hadn't occurred to him to think of.

"No, I am not going out with that girl that I met yesterday at the disco party," said Robert, his lanky redheaded room-mate, "my girlfriend is waiting in my home town for me. I am not going to do that to her."

"Really?" loudly laughed the other boys, "and when did you start to be such a faithful guy?"

Passing moments 16 (1980).

Rose attended the same university as Julo in a different department. She was one year older and lived in the same dormitory, only in a separate portion of the building where no males were allowed after 10pm. She was blonde, nice, a little bit round-faced and had a beautiful, nicely shaped body. When Rose smiled she displayed two small holes in her cheeks, and she was always smiling. When she talked she laughed and smiled at the same time. When she talked to Julo, it was not only her smile that he liked.

It was the way that when she had something important to say, she gently touched his shoulder.

An attractive young woman, she knew how to enjoy and get as much out of her life as possible. Rose somehow sensed that Julo was a sexually inexperienced boy. Rose was not. She once told Julo how she protected herself against pregnancy. She always carried with her a small, sharp pin; the kind one sticks into a cork board to attach paper. She had that pin in her purse and she had the purse next to her, even when she was being undressed by her 'one-time' boyfriend. When she and her boyfriend got into the intimate position, she quietly took the pin into her hand so her boyfriend wouldn't notice. When they were enjoying sexual intercourse she paid attention. She watched and tried not to miss the moment when man got to his flashpoint. She learned to recognize that moment, and a second before it came, she would not hesitate; she would stab the small, sharp pin into the boy's bum!

Julo laughed loudly when Rose described what usually happened next.

"He jumps out of me like space rocket 3, 2, 1 and blast off...ha ha ha! Julo, do you want to try that?"

Life-time moments, life-time questions; those moments rarely occur again; but they stick with you forever.

"Umm..." Julo was caught by surprise; faithfulness ran through his mind.

"Can I take a rain check?" he asked, squirming a little.

Rose smiled, "Yes, you can, no expiration date. You are dumb as girls are saying..."

Passing moments 17 (1980).

The first university summer break was almost there. Julo decided to surprise Lea. He found a job during the summer break and earned enough money to pay for a one-week stay for two at a famous mountain resort. They both were excited and looked forward to the trip.

Before the trip Lea went to visit her aunt in the capital city Bratislava for 3 weeks. They wrote letters to each other while she was away, expressing how much they missed each other. Lea described in her letters the good time she was having, meeting new friends and going to disco parties with them. In one of the letters she wrote:

"I wish you were here with us. We went to the famous club in Bratislava's downtown. There was a marathon dancing competition. Jozo, who lives next door to my aunt, asked me to be his partner in it. He is a dance instructor so I agreed. That night I was so exhausted. The competition started at 8:00pm and lasted four hours. In the short breaks Jozo had to put ice on my face. The best part was rock-and-roll. He took me into his arms like in 'Saturday Night Fever'. Imagine at the end, there were only about five dancing couples and then we won! Jozo took me home in his car afterwards. How I wished you were there and could dance with me."

Julo finished reading Lea's letter. His Pandora brain box unlocked and released huge streams of jealousy. If someone wants to be in love, he must know that this ingredient goes together with the bohemian love feeling. This uncompromised feeling of jealousy started to pound on Julo in heavy doses. Jealousy started to be an indivisible part of Julo's nightly torments.

Finally at the end of August Julo and Lea packed their hiking stuff and took a train to the mountain resort. During the day they hiked. During the night when they were together in bed, Julo tried to do what was written into his gene code; to try for reproduction. Lea's gene codes however (in that moment of her life) were outputting: *'no, not now'*. The week in the mountain resort ended with no change in their virginity status.

Passing moments 18 (1981).

The second year of university study, the third year of Julo and Lea's relationship. They still enjoyed each other's company. Lea, now a senior in high school, didn't know what she would do after her high school years were over. They spent more time studying together so she would get better grades, in case she would apply for college or university. Lea talked more and more about going somewhere far away after high school. Julo knew he couldn't change the path of their relationship, no matter how much he would like to try to do so.

Lea decided to execute their break shortly before their third year dating anniversary and so their relationship ended with the same virginity status as it had started. Julo tried a few times to salvage their relationship, before he finally acknowledged Lea's decision and started to live with the new fact.

When Julo's friends in dormitory learned about Julo and Lea's break soon after it happened, they engaged Julo in their student/dormitory life a little bit more than they did before. Julo noticed that the '*gloomy kind of buns*' were mixing into his night thoughts quite frequently now. He knew those thoughts were the same kind of thoughts that he was playing with when he was small kid (who would be crying about when he would die); they were the same kind of sneaky self-pity thoughts manufactured by hell and thus should yet be put in a cage with heavy metal rods and kept locked forever. Julo didn't yet know that this was exactly what he would have to learn to do.

He started to do more sports than he did before. He played tennis more frequently and he loved his biking trips more and more: to sit on his bike and go away for hours. He still couldn't wait until the weekend came to hurry back home; perhaps he would see Lea by accident. Two months after their official break they did.

"Hi," she said, looking just beyond his shoulder.

"Hi," he replied carefully.

They walked together in drizzling rain, talked about general stuff. Then it started to rain harder so they stopped to protect themselves under the bus station roof.

Julo suddenly asked, "are you still virgin?"

Lea looked at him, then turned towards misted bus station window and wrote with her finger "no".

Julo's heart started to pound. He didn't dare ask who it was, where it was, what music was playing, whether all her dreamed expectations of how this special moment of her life should be were fulfilled. He left without saying anything. The sarcastic joke that his cousin liked to say came to his mind: "*there are two types of tarts: regular tarts and exceptional tarts; a regular tart goes with every man; an exceptional tart goes with everybody except you.*"

Passing moments 19 (1983).

Julo was now in the fourth year of studying at university, just one more year and he would get his Master's degree and be done with the graduate study. He had been avoiding having a long relationship with any girl. He felt betrayed and didn't think that he would be able to fall in love again. He had done something to one girl that he was now ashamed of.

Mirriam and Maja were good friends, both very beautiful, both attending gymnastic classes. They were both 17, while Julo was now 22. Julo liked Mirriam, but she was not really paying attention to him. Maja was though. So Julo asked Maja for a date, she agreed (Mirriam would not; he was almost sure about that). Julo had two dates with Maja. They kissed and enjoyed touching each other (nothing more). Julo liked the small ordeal but didn't want to continue on to a bigger relationship. He would perhaps with Mirriam. He didn't say anything to Maja after those two dates, he simply hid himself at home as a mouse would hide in a mouse hole and thought that by not going into the outside world all would be forgotten. He stayed home (his mom liked that) and didn't go out for several months.

His cousin Stanley asked him, "Julo, what you have done to Maja?! She is so much in love with you! She now comes to the club each night hoping to see you… and you are hiding at home!" His cousin smiled at him.

Julo felt bad. Those kisses were good. He felt miserable though; he should not have just kissed and retreated. Later on he looked at this episode with different eyes (a sweet feeling) and hoped that Maja would also remember those two nights same way as he did.

Julo created his 'mouse hole' and found out that this a good place to hide. He ran into that hole whenever his conscience (superego) told him that he had done something wrong. Then he would come to the edge of the hole to check out what was going on in the outside world. Nothing! Nobody cared that he kissed a girl he didn't want to date. He came slowly out of the hole to see that the same girl he thought he made miserable was smiling at him. After a couple of months Maja met another guy who she started to date. Julo noticed that they held hands nonstop, 24/7. *Nothing against holding hands,* he thought, *but 24/7?* It wasn't any of his business anyway; they could hold hands as much as they chose so.

Passing moments 20 (1984).

Julo was in his fifth and last year of study before he got his master's degree. Those *'gloomy kind of bun'* thoughts were not going away; indeed they now came almost every night before he fell asleep; gloomy thoughts, with a mix of self pity, they became his night time heroin. Julo connected those thoughts with Lea leaving him and betraying his love. He had more migraine-type headaches that had become more and more unbearable.

Around that time Vladimir Levi's book *"The Art of Being Yourself"* fell into Julo's hands. He read the book and was hypnotized by its content. The uncontrolled self-pity thoughts must stop and Levi's book was going to help him. His logic told him that it took about three years for him to get to his current state so it shouldn't take more than three years to get out of it. The book was a great introduction to Julo's knowledge about human psychology, consciousness, unconsciousness, and most particularly about how to control his thoughts and inner life.

What is a brain anyway? A bunch of neurons that somehow connect to each other with a special type of connection called synapses. So there are hundreds of billions of cells, each cell linked to tens of thousands of other brain cells. Wouldn't be cool if there was an extra internal switch that would control the way brain reacts?

Stop, this chain of self-pitying thoughts are not permitted!

Yes, this chain reaction was the one I liked; that was a happy feeling; again how it was triggered?

Stop, not in the past, not in the future, just in the current moment.

Hm, what else is very interesting there? '*Love yourself as you love your fellow man.*' He heard that very often when he attended Sunday mass when he was a boy. He remembered that Father Komornik said often during his mass '*Love your fellow man.*' He didn't remember though saying '*Love yourself as you would love your fellow man.*'

Yes, this is what I should do, Julo thought. He believed he put his love for Lea ahead of love for himself. *Was that the reason she betrayed me?* went through Julo's mind. *Stop, this thought is not permitted!* Julo gave himself a smile. Julo started implementing his inner switch.

Every great thing happens slowly. No rush, no need for that. He started to regularly practice Autogenous Training (AT), which was originally developed by German psychiatrist Schultz and was described in great detail in Levi's book. Julo lay on the bed; his breathing became deeper, he closed his eyes and started slowly focusing on his muscles:

Head: relax muscles on the forehead, cheeks, around the mouth, the chin, all the muscles in my head are relaxed now;

Shoulder, relax muscles in both shoulders;

Focus on the right arm, relax muscles there, relax the muscles around the elbow and in the right hand, all the right arm is relaxed now;

Go to the left arm; relax the muscles there, relax the muscles around the elbow and in the left hand, all the left arm is relaxed now;

Focus on the back; relax the muscles in the back; go down to pelvis, relax muscles there;

Focus on the right leg, go slowly down, relax each muscle there; all the muscles in the right leg are relaxed now;

Focus on the left leg; go slowly down, relax each muscle there; all the muscles in the left leg are relaxed now;

At this stage Julo started saying to himself, *I am completely relaxed now; I am breathing slowly, deeply; every muscle in my body is relaxed; I am going back...* then:

Tense the muscles in the left leg; slowly from the foot up;

Tense the muscles in the right leg; slowly from the foot up;

Tense the muscles in the back; tense muscles in the left hand;

Go up from the fingers to the neck;

Tense the muscles in the right hand;

Go up from the fingers to the neck; tense the neck, tense the muscles on the face;

Open the eyes; stand up...

To go from the start to complete relaxation and back took Julo about 15 minutes; sometimes he fell asleep and woke up 20-30 minutes later. Julo practiced AT at the end of his final year at the University of Kosice; after two-three months he learned to go from one muscle to another on one breath-in, breath-out. After six months of practicing AT (when he graduated from university) he could bring a warm feeling into his arms and legs; after nine months of daily practice (when he enlisted in the Air Force at Hradec Kralove) he could bring heaviness into his body. He took all Levi's books with him when he moved from his home-town to Hradec Kralove.

<u>Passing moments 21 (1985).</u>

Julo was now serving his country at the Hradec Kralove Air-force complex. He thought how lucky he was to be in a room with only nine soldiers, rather than a big one crowded with 25 as most soldiers were. The soldiers sharing a room with him were fine young boys.

"Julo, how you can fall to sleep so easily when we have a break?" Jirka asked him, "you guys from Slovakia are so funny. One is always writing something; the other is always sleeping."

"I don't sleep, Jirko. I am practicing AT," Julo explained.

"Practicing what?" Jirko's laugh was contagious.

"AT is Autogenous Training; you learn to control your muscles by relaxing and tensing them."

"But why? What is this good for?" asked Jirka with a quizzical look on his face.

Julo didn't want to go into the real reason he had started practicing AT.

"You learn to control yourself; first you learn to relax each muscle in your body; then you learn to get warmth into each part of your body. After you master that you can learn to get a heavy feeling into arms and legs..."

"Really? Warmth? Heavy feeling?" Jirko interrupted. He didn't want to believe it; he was just smiling and rolling his eyes, "how you do that?"

"Jirko, here is the book. If you are interested, please read it."

"Noo. I am not too much into reading."

"I've got an idea, Jirko. Do you really want to know what I am doing? I will show you. Please lie down on the bed, make yourself comfortable and follow my sentences as I am going to tell you what you should do."

"Ha, you would hypnotize me and ask stupid questions and then you would laugh at me..."

"No, Jirko, don't worry. I promise I would not do that."

Jirka agreed. He lay on the bed, closed his eyes and followed what Julo told him to do; he followed Julo's way of relaxing each muscle, starting from the head all the way down to the feet. When Julo saw that Jirko was relaxed and breathing almost as he would if asleep, he continued with an easy voice, "your body is completely relaxed. Imagine you are lying on the beach under a tree, you are comfortable, breathing deeply..." Julo saw Jirka's deep breath in and breath out, "you can hear the hiss of the ocean.

You are now lying in a boat on the ocean, you can feel how the boat goes up, and goes down. When it goes down you feel that gravity has ceased to exist, again the boat goes up... and now down... You are enjoying this moment very much... you are back on the beach. And you focus now on the muscles in the legs, put the tension there, put the tension in the muscles of the upper body, breath in, breath out, tension in the muscles of both hands and on the face. You are awakening... open the eyes, you are up..."

Jirko opened his eyes and smiled, "that was good! I was sleeping but heard your voice; where was I? I was on the boat; that was cool. You Slovak guys... I like you so much. Let's go for a beer. The three of us, you, Jozef and I."

"Agreed," said Julo.

Passing moments 22 (1985).

After finishing reading Levi's books Julo turned to Buddha's and yoga type books. He found lot of similarities there. He started to put things together. He was thinking about his self-confidence and interest about himself. It caught his attention how those two things correlate and compared this to his behavior. *Self-confidence and interest about yourself. How are other people expressing interest about themselves? When does this good feeling after hearing ordinary praise turn into possession? Do I really want to learn what other people are saying about me? Is this what is decreasing my own self-confidence? The more you are interested in what kind of attitude others are expressing about you, the lower your self-confidence. And vice versa. The more you try genuinely to be interested about somebody else your self-confidence rise. Easy like that! Problem of self-confidence resolved! Hm...*

Julo then turned his thinking towards his doubt about himself; doubt about his abilities were built deeply into him. He started to realize that he was putting too much weight on others' judgment of his abilities. His self-confidence was low and the reason could be his craving to hear praise from somebody else: *I have to stop trying to find out what other people are saying about me! Or even better, not care at all about what people are saying.* Julo thought he had to do that: turn the interest outside towards others and try to selflessly give something to somebody else.

What about the power of giving? Encouragement about selfless giving could be found in Buddha's teaching or in Jesus's teaching; just read the books. Does that power correlate to your self-confidence as well? It does. The power of giving, the power of genuine giving, wise giving raises the level of your self-confidence …thoughts that were zipping in Julo's mind.

Whenever there was free time Julo either read books or practiced AT. It had been over a year now that he had been practicing AT each day for at least 20-30 minutes and he could see the results. AT works, works for him at least. He was convinced that the things he read in the books are true. The migraine type of headache, which he noticed at the end of his graduate study went away. He also noticed improvement of his memory.

And the time in *kasarne* was flying for him quickly. The waste of time while you are fulfilling your mandatory serving (a complaint that he heard so often) didn't apply to him. Julo could now bring the feeling of warmth or heaviness into his arms and legs. He liked his AT sessions. He knew it would take time to master them. No hurry, slowly. The power was in the peace and calmness. Julo's elementary math teacher had noticed Julo's rush to do things fast. When he had asked him to give math lesson to his fellow students (what grade it was? so many years ago) he reminded him not to hurry and then the same math teacher added at the front of all the class after lecturing Julo not to do anything hasty: "Don't run to catch bus or after a girl… in 15 minutes another comes…"

What Julo had not considered as important (while reading books he liked very much), were sentences about inner anger. He didn't pay attention when he read a quote from Nikolai Gogol, dramatist, novelist of Ukrainian-Polish ethnicity about inner anger in one of Levi's book. He never thought that this was something that could derail thinking to it's darkness trails. The inside anger was not inside him, not in the way that Julo would realize and notice it was there. No need to pay attention to it.

Julo liked Levi's idea about trying to find somewhere inside—the 'mood switch' that generated happiness—and turn this switch on as often as possible. A good start would be to learn to appreciate small daily things and events and rejoice before they happen, when they are happening and after they have happened; and to do that again and again. For example, displaying joy in walking. Learn to synchronize breathing, inhale slowly and deeply, keep the breath in, so oxygen gets into the blood system and exhale even slower. Learn to focus, point the eyes at some object and keep focus; don't let anything disrupt the focus.

It is one thing is to collect information and another to implement it into the daily life; start and never stop. If you don't continue, if you don't remind yourself to do it again and again it is as if you didn't start. You read this at a certain age, you think you understand the importance of what you read, you practice that for while, then stop, forget about it; then your life has to give you one blow, another and another; remind you go back what you read in the past and realize the importance idea 'never stop'. You can restart, of course, what else? Restart, don't stop and you find out that it is true: you have to change yourself to understand yourself.

There are thousands and thousands synapses that link one cell with other brain cells; rewiring is a time-taking process; disconnect and reconnect those cells requires not only inside determination but also creating a good physical environment so cells would reconnect the way you desire. It's like soldering copper wire to the motherboard, you have to have a certain temperature and you have to have a brazing solder, which melts and connects copper to the motherboard. Brazing solder would be food that you supply to your body; correct temperature would be right amount of that food, at the right time to supply that food. Meaning eat three or four times a day, mostly vegetables and fish, less frequently red meat; avoid sugar and sweet products, do yoga type of body cleaning once a week. Body cleaning? Yes, body cleaning: eating nothing for certain time period (for example 24 hours) and making sure to drink lots of water during that time period. Preparing the body before and slowly getting body to regular habits after is as important as the fasting time period: a good example could be to eat just fruit the day before and after the 24 hours of fasting.

Julo tried all this, determined to change himself and adopt a different, new lifestyle.

Passing moments 23 (1985).

After serving six months in the army Julo was promoted to a higher rank: second lieutenant. As a lieutenant he could go out of the *kasarne* without requesting a special permit, *opustak*, which generally was not easy to obtain. Julo could go to the pub and drink with other soldiers that received *opustak*. That was not his style however. He didn't like to sit in the pub, drink beer and talk about girls. He would rather go to the cinema and he saw several movies each weekend. Even after that he still had more spare time outside of the *kasarne*. What else he could do?

There was nice aquatic center in Hradec Kralove with a sauna and steam room. Next to the sauna room there were two small ponds, 4 feet by 4 feet, with cold and hot water. The cold water was really cold, icy water. In his home town, Presov, when he got overheated in the sauna, Julo had loved to jump into the icy cold water of the pond. He felt the needles on his skin as he switched between cold and hot water and back again and enjoyed it.

He thought perhaps he could harden himself with the cold water. He decided to slowly train his body to withstand the icy water for three, four, or even more, minutes. His plan was that he would go every Wednesday evening and every weekend to the town and train his body. He thought about who would go with him. Jirka or Jozef couldn't go with him - they wouldn't get a permit to go out of the *kasarne* every weekend and besides, they liked to go to pub when they did get one. So, he would go there by himself. It would be better if he could go there with a friend, no big deal though.

Julo went to aquatic center at least twice a week and slowly increased his time in the icy water. In the third week he stayed for two minutes. In the fourth week he made it to 2.5 minutes. By the fifth week he was doing three minutes and at week six, 3.5 minutes.

Brr, this water is cold to my bones, Julo thought, but he didn't give up. His goal was to stay in the cold icy water for 5 minutes. He now had sympathy for the life of polar bears and he wasn't sure whether five minutes would be too much!

It was winter-time; the beginning of the year and the weather outside the pool was cold too. Finally, after eight weeks, he decided to abandon this crazy idea to train his body for cold water and he stopped going to the aquatic center. He was now always cold and he thought he should see a doctor.

"So, you've got a cold and you think you have a fever too?" the army doctor asked Julo when he came to see him.

"Yes, comrade doctor."

"Well, in this cold weather it is not surprise. Your body temperature is quite high. I would rather you stay here in the army hospital for a week or so until your temperature goes down a little bit. It's too high," he said shaking his head.

Passing moments 24 (1985).

Julo was in the army hospital in Hradec Kralove. He didn't feel like there was any difference whether he was in the *kasarne* or in the army hospital. He felt OK – he didn't know why they had decided to keep him in the hospital. The army doctors didn't tell him much. He just had to stay in the hospital.

The doctor came by his bed one cool morning.

"Comrade Second Lieutenant, we have to transfer you to the general army hospital in Prague! Two weeks have passed and your body temperature is still high, even after the antibiotics cure. There must be something else. We don't know what and we don't want to take a chance. You will be transferred tomorrow morning," he said with a brief nod of his head.

Go to the army hospital in Prague! That could be fun. Julo liked the idea – it was known to be the biggest hospital in the whole of Czechoslovakia. Not everybody got to go to that hospital. It treated famous people; actors, artists, even the president of Czechoslovakia went there for his treatment! And Julo is going to be treated there as well!

Julo arrived in the army hospital in Prague to find that life in a hospital room with soldiers being treated is not the same as life for civilians in hospital. If a doctor (who was also a colonel) entered the room of soldiers, the highest-ranking soldier had to give an official report. In this case, Julo gave the report.

"Attention, Comrade Colonel, I obediently report that all is OK, present are two soldiers, nobody is missing". He and the two other soldiers in the same room stood solid like iron in their army pajamas. *The colonel must have fun observing and participating in this morning ceremony as we do; who would take this comedy seriously?* Julo thought.

Doctor Colonel replied, "Thank you Comrade Second Lieutenant, you all can sit on your beds now."

The doctor checked the records of Julo's illness.

"Comrade Second Lieutenant, we have to send you to specialists. Your blood sedimentation indicates that there is something serious somewhere in your body. We have to find the source. I don't want to frighten you but usually a body with cancer responds with this kind of blood sedimentation. It is serious."

Over the course of the next few days, Julo saw every possible specialist: one for eyes, one for ears, one for head, stomach, legs. Each of them asked questions, took an x-ray and each of them tried to find some kind of malicious tumor, the source of the high sedimentation in Julo's blood. Meantime, Julo felt OK, except that he was always cold. He didn't complain about his cold, in fact he rarely complained about anything. He certainly didn't reveal the eight-week body-hardening plan that he finished about a month ago. He thought that by revealing what he had done he would expose his stupidity. He felt OK and he had fun in the hospital; there were young nurses here. He could chat and joke with them. Time went much faster in Prague compared with Hradec Kralove.

In his third week in the army hospital around 10am Julo went to the cafeteria to buy some snacks. Standing in the line waiting for his turn to order, suddenly he felt his legs collapsing and he fainted, losing consciousness. He didn't know where he was. He felt nothing; blank. How long was the blankness there? He doesn't know. Then his consciousness came back. *Where am I?* Julo wondered. *Back in my hospital room. How did I get here? I went to buy a snack in the cafeteria!*

"Comrade Second Lieutenant, can you see me?"

Who is asking that question? Oo, it is a doctor colonel.

"Yes, I can see you," Julo replied.

"Your body collapsed, you were without consciousness for about two hours."

Interesting, Julo speculated, *so this is how death feels? The mind stops working, legs collapse and there is nothing; complete blankness. Was I really dying and then suddenly my body didn't want to give up and woke me up? Was it my body or my mind? After two hours my willingness to live wins and my mind and body starts to work again? Interesting.*

After the loss of consciousness things suddenly started to change. It was like the body gave itself 'all-or-nothing' choices: 'all' meaning everything gets back to normal, 'nothing' meaning the body would dissolve itself in high blood sedimentation. The body chose 'all'; it woke up from unconsciousness and decided to be completely OK. The body's decision on which way to go took several hours and after that all Julo's blood tests showed normal results.

"Comrade Second Lieutenant, you have been here for four weeks. The blood tests were abnormal the first three weeks. Last week after you fainted and then woke up, and suddenly the blood test results have been looking good. We don't know what happened. We don't know why you got those alarming blood test results. We don't know what got them back to normal. It was probably an unusual high fever. The bottom line is we are going to send you back to Hradec Kralove."

"Thank you, comrade colonel," Julo replied. He never told doctor that he knows why he got the unusual high fever.

"You are welcome comrade second lieutenant," the Colonel replied.

Passing moments 25 (1986).

When Julo's year in the *kasarne* of Hradec Kralove ended he went back to his home-town, Presov, and started work for a company that focused on the research and development of robots and robotic parts. He was part of a computer programming team and was assigned challenging tasks, which he enjoyed. In his free time he played tennis or he biked.

During his first summer vacation Julo, together with two of his friends, went to a 14-day tennis camp in Czech town Pardubice, where he met Renata. Renata liked Julo. Julo liked Renata. He liked the cleverness hidden inside of her, which she exposed only in particular moments.

"It was my first time," Renata told Julo after the first night they spent together.

"And you didn't make big deal out of it?" asked Julo.

"Should I?" smiled Renata at Julo.

Julo didn't tell Renata that it was his first time too.

No earthquake type of experience, as Hemingway described in one of his books. No specially designed evening with a designated song that would be remembered forever (as Lea dreamed to have).

<u>Passing moments 26 (1987).</u>

Julo thought it was time to buy his first car and he saved enough money to purchase a used Skoda 105.

"Julo, why do you want to buy a used car? You will spend lots of time on repairs. Tell me how much money you would need to buy new one?"

Is this my father asking me? wondered Julo. Julo's father could be generous but not usually to his closest family members. He was known for ordering drinks for everybody in the pub, and he didn't forget to praise himself for this act. He did this only when he was drunk; never when he was sober.

But his father was serious. Julo accepted his dad's gift and bought new Skoda 105. He adored his car and it became his second home. He could put a bike in it and drive somewhere far away where he could then ride, together with his thoughts.

<u>Passing moments 27 (1988).</u>

Julo decided to practice days free of any food because he believed it was the way to get rid of his dark thoughts, and eventually make his life happier. He started with practicing a half-day without food every week. He did this for a month, then increased to one day each week. On the third month of his fasting experience Julo decided to try three full days.

It was summer. Julo took several bottles of water, put his tent in his Skoda 105 and left for a three-day hiking trip without any food. The first two days went quite quickly. The worst was the third day; he felt that he didn't have enough power for walking, his orientation abilities changed to orientation disabilities and he had to think hard not to get lost in the woods. He made it though, survived three days without any food.

He then slowly got back to normal eating, which turned out to be the hardest part. His appetite was big and it was very hard for him to control the amount of food he wanted to put into his stomach. His body changed rapidly.

"Julo, is that you?" several friends said, "you look so bad, like you just came out of a concentration camp."

Passing moments 28 (1989).

After four years of working in the research and development company, Julo had to look for another work opportunity. All companies in former Czechoslovak Socialist Republic were under government control. The 'Velvet' revolution of December 1989 put an end to a lot of companies, including the research company where Julo worked.

Julo thought he may leave his home town or even his country, though he didn't know exactly where he would go or what he would do. He just didn't want to stay in his home town. His friend David told him about a work opportunity in Prague, in a completely different field: construction.

Julo and Dave had worked together on several small construction projects during Julo's summer breaks from university. So Julo decided to go to Prague, initially for just two weeks. He worked for a big construction company building estate housing, *Cerny Most*. He was in charge of a group of seasonal workers mostly from Slovakia, Poland or Ukraine. He earned decent money but was not happy with the type of work he was doing.

He still liked to go home to be with his family and friends.

"Julo, how is life in Prague?" asked his neighbor Ander when Julo walked home one Saturday afternoon.

"It's OK," replied Julo.

"Come in, Julo. Would you mind helping me move some heavy stuff in the backyard?"

This was not the first time that Julo helped Ander and his wife Jolca. They had a good neighbor-to-neighbor relationship. Ander and Jolca were in their fifties, didn't have kids and they liked to have Julo come over for small chats. Ander worked at state-run farm (UAA; United Agriculturalist Alliance) as a tractor driver. Another tractor driver who worked there, Ilja, moved from Russia about seven years ago. Ilja was likeable guy, in a similar way to Ander.

Ander gossiped, "You know that Ilja takes his lunch break at Ilona's house more often? Ilona's husband looks like a man without a soul, walking like a rain-swept rooster, and Ilona is full of life; she wants a man in her bed! I don't envy Ilja. He is doing what Ilona's husband ought to do. I only wish I could do that!"

Julo listened, not saying anything.

"Julo, you know, there are so many nice women in the UAA," said Ander. Then he paused briefly before his monolog continued with a surprise revealing, "my instrument doesn't want to get up anymore…"

Julo was not sure whether he was hearing what he was hearing; he looked at Jolca who was sitting next to Ander. Jolca smiled and tried to stop Ander's monolog.

But he continued, "I don't know what happened. I want him to get up but when it comes to it… he doesn't." Ander's right fist gently hit his open left palm.

Julo didn't understand why Ander (who was much older than he was) was telling him this. Julo's thoughts came back to Ander's revealing monolog several times later in his life. Were Ander and Jolca giving a completely different meaning to their sexual life? Were they giving to this human act, designed for reproduction, a completely different meaning? Were they raising its importance to the stratosphere, and did all this then backfire to Ander's bedroom performance? Was there a similarity between Jolca and Lea in their dreaming of how this act should be and that putting too much weight on this ordinary act?

Passing moments 29 (1990).

Julo liked his new Prague residence; he lived in an apartment belonging to the construction company for which he worked. He didn't like the evenings when he came home to his empty apartment; nobody waiting for him, nobody with whom he could share the experiences of his day. His thoughts returned to Lea; wondering what she was doing. No, he would never try to find out where she was; he would not even admit that he would like to know. She had betrayed him; he would not forgive that, not at this point of his life.

The loneliness was killing him. He met Erzsha—a nice girl with long black hair—in a train when he was traveling from Prague to his home town. Erzsha was from Kosice, had finished high school two years ago and now worked as a receptionist in a hotel. They exchanged addresses and started to write each other. After three months of mail communication and several dates, Julo invited Erzsha to come to Prague to live with him.

Passing moments 30 (1991).

Julo was now working for TSR (Ted Sekera Remodeling). Ted Sekera was a 52-year-old building contractor who immigrated to Austria in 1968 with his wife and three-year-old daughter. Like all other immigrants in 1968-69 he thought he would never get back to his home country Czechoslovakia. Ted learned construction working for several companies. Later he started his own construction business doing remodeling work, mostly in Austria, but also in other western European countries. After communism collapsed in Czechoslovakia in 1989 and later both Czech Republic and Slovakia were included in the Eurozone, Ted expanded his business to Czech Republic.

Ted hired Julo as a regular construction worker around the same time Erzsha moved to Prague to share the apartment with Julo. Ted saw that Julo possessed good manual skills and good logical thinking and thought that Julo could eventually run his business in Czech Republic. TSR had only a few permanent employees. When TSR got a contract for a project in a city, Ted moved there with two-three permanent employees and they then hired temporary local workers who did most of the work until the project was completed. Ted and Julo spent lots of hours together, traveling by car from one project to another, or staying in motels until the project was completed. One night in a motel, reclining back in a faded old chair near the TV, Ted told Julo his life story.

"Yes, some people escaped from communist Czechoslovakia because they were oppressed by the communist regime, but most of them escaped because they wanted to experience something else; they were not allowed to see how the western world looked like, so when the situation in 1968 allowed them to escape the country they decided to leave and try this different world," he declared as he smoothed out one of his unruly eyebrows, "I tell you something though, Julo. When any woman that grew up in Czechoslovakia during the communist regime moves to the west, she gets some kind of mental disorder. I don't know any couple that escaped from our country that didn't divorced later. Every woman who gets to the west goes crazy; she starts to think that the western style of life means cheating on their husbands."

Julo looked at Ted, he was serious. Ted continued.

"My ex-wife did the same to me. She could at least have chosen someone better looking, a little bit more intelligent! No, she didn't, she chose a man from the lowest scum; some Middle-eastern emigrant working as restaurant cleaner." Julo saw the rage on Ted's face. Ted then told Julo that he divorced his wife. All women became pigs for Ted.

Ted liked to exaggerate things. His friend once said, "When Ted tells you something, you need to use a 1:2 or 1:3 correlation to get little bit closer to the correctness of his claim. For example, if he tells you that he is earning $200,000.00 a year, it means that he earns between $65,000.00 and $100,000.00. If he tells you he has dated 10 girls in past two months, he probably had a date with two or three girls in last 6-8 months. If he tells you he has run a marathon, he perhaps ran 2 or 5 km."

Julo remembered this and smiled to himself while listening to Ted's stories.

"I can get any woman I choose; there is no escape for her. When she starts dating me that is it for her. She would enjoy our time together so much that when we split she will never be happy again. What? You are laughing? "asked Ted.

"No, no I am not," answered Julo. For Julo (now 29) it was strange to learn that a 50-year-old man would date girls the way Julo thought teenagers or boys in their twenties would do.

Ted knew how to bid for the projects and how to win them. He didn't know how to keep money or wisely spend the money he earned.

"Look here at this check," Ted showed Julo a $100,000.00 check he received as a down-payment for their next project. He smiled from ear to ear. Later that same day he asked Julo to keep an eye on the project and told him he would be gone for one week. Ted bought himself and his new girlfriend a one-week vacation stay in a Greek resort. Ted spent money quickly; perhaps that was the main reason he didn't pay his employees and the project subcontractors. Ted chose whom to pay, and who not. Julo, thankfully, was in the paid category; Ted paid Julo all the money he earned working for TSR.

Passing moments 31 (1992).

It was at the end of the summer when Erzsha moved to Prague to share the apartment with Julo. Julo didn't ask Erzsha to pay any part of the rent

57

and Erzsha didn't ask whether she should contribute; and if she had, Julo would have said that she didn't have to pay. Erzsha made the apartment cozy, adding a few pictures on the wall and a few vases to the corners of the room. She liked to keep the apartment clean and all had to be in order.

"Julo, come here please," Julo came and look at Erzsha; she was pointing to the floor.

"What is that?"

"My socks," Julo replied, a little sheepishly.

"I just cleaned all the rooms 10 minutes ago. Didn't you notice that?"

"...and..." Julo tried with a smile.

"And you make this apartment look messy. Look into your closet! I put everything in order there two days ago. It's so messy now! You should see my father's closet! Umm, I guess not all men are as clean and organized as my father is! Take those socks and put them where they belong!"

Julo didn't like Erzsha's authoritative tone at all. It irritated him, created anger inside. He didn't say anything though; he just took the socks and threw them into the basket.

Erzsha grew up in a strong Catholic environment. In Kosice she used to attend every Sunday mass and she continued to do so when she moved to Prague. Julo grew up in a Catholic family as well. Still, it was strange to him that a young girl in her twenties was so devotedly religious. He went a few times to Sunday mass with Erzsha; later on he skipped the Sunday mass more often.

Passing moments 32 (1992).

Julo told Ted about Erzsha three weeks after she arrived. Ted's first question was whether she had a job.

"No, she doesn't," Julo told Ted.

"She can work with us. We can find her work on our projects. I also need help with my paperwork. Tell her she can start work with us next week."

So, now Julo and Erzsha were both living and working together. Julo did all kinds of carpentry work, framing, drywall, electrical work. Erzsha learnt some carpentry work as well, and she could now hang wallpaper, do some painting work. On Saturdays she cleaned Ted's apartment and did some office work for Ted while she was there. The company's projects were often far away from Prague. Places like Poland, Germany or Austria. They stayed there for a week or two and came back to Prague for the weekends. They both had fun with Ted and started to use Ted's vocabulary.

"Julo, watch, what you would say about those two pigs standing on the corner of the street? Ted would like them, don't you think so?" Erzsha was pointing to two street-walkers.

"Ted likes all kind of pigs. I guess he would like those as well."

Passing moments 33 (1993).

Julo and Erzsha celebrated six months living together in same apartment.

"Julo, last time I was home in Kosice my mom told me that we shouldn't live like this." After short pause Erzsha continued, "She said that we should either get married or I should go back home to Kosice," she said tucking her hair behind her ear.

"Hm, so your mom is pressuring you to get married before your older sister does?" asked Julo.

"Well, yes she is…"

Julo had been thinking about getting married. He would be 30 years old next year. He remembered how people in small towns, or in small neighborhoods in bigger towns, could pressure younger fellows to get married.

He remembered walking down the street in his home town two years ago when his elementary math teacher stopped him and told him, "Julo, how come you are still single? That is not the way to live life! You are like my son, who is two years older than you are. He lives the same way! You should get married!"

Julo was surprised by his elementary math teacher's verbal attack. He was not expecting that at all and was not sure whether math teacher was serious at first. He was…

Passing moments 34 (1993).

It was the beginning of February, still cold, and the streets were covered with more than 10 inches of snow. Julo had to go to Slovakia. His mom

59

fell off the steps, got seriously injured and was in the hospital. He thought he would need to stay in Slovakia for at least two weeks. Ted didn't agree to give both of them two weeks of vacation, so Erzsha stayed in Prague while Julo went home.

Two weeks passed quickly. Julo was glad that he could see his mom; the injury was not life-threatening thankfully because at her age these types of injuries could have serious consequences. While he was home he did a little bit of shopping. Julo had decided to buy Erzsha an engagement ring and propose on Valentine's Day.

"What kind of ring should I buy for my fiancée-to-be?" Julo asked the young saleslady in the jewelry store with a smile.

"Do you know what her lucky stone is?" she asked from behind the counter top.

"No, I don't. What would be the most memorable type of the ring?"

"I would say sapphires. We have a gorgeous sapphire-diamond ring or you could choose from such precious stones as emeralds or rubies or just a little bit less precious such as this aquamarine ring or this..."

"Which one you would like to get?" Julo looked directly into the saleslady's eyes and enjoyed the blush on her cheeks.

"Well, if I was in this memorable moment of my life, I think any of these rings would make me happy; but... since I guess you want to hear which one I would choose... it would be the sapphire ring..."

Of course, Julo thought, *the most expensive one.*

"OK, I am going to buy that one then," Julo said. He didn't like to spend too much time in any store, and he did the same thing now, bought the first one recommended to him.

Passing moments 35 (1993).

On the train back to Prague Julo thought about how and when he should give the ring to Erzsha. Valentine's Day was on Sunday. He thought they could go to a restaurant somewhere downtown, then they would take a walk on Charles Bridge and he would give Erzsha the ring there and ask her to marry him. He didn't notice any excitement while thinking of it. *So what,* he thought, *sometimes important life events come and go without a special type of excitement.*

It was Friday evening when he opened his apartment door and Erzsha was not home. She probably just stepped out of the apartment to do some shopping, Julo thought. He then saw an envelope and an open letter lying on the kitchen desk. He looked at the envelope; the sender was Nora, Erzsha's older sister. He started to read the letter without touching it and his heart started to pump heavily right after he read the first two sentences.

> *Dear sis Erzshika,*
> *I was so excited to receive the last letter from you; I couldn't wait until I would plunge again into your sentences describing your relationship with Ted. I am soo happy for you. If you are sure you love Ted you don't have to have any qualms. You live your life just once; enjoy it. Just remember to either take some anti-pregnancy pills or have condoms with you when you go to visit Ted in his apartment. You don't want to get pregnant so soon. Even though the way you describing Ted he could be your life partner. Oo I am little bit jealous. Do I understand correctly? He wants to take you for two weeks vacation to Italy? Hahaha and he thought that Valentine's Day was February 4th and gave you beautiful roses thinking that it was Valentine's Day. That is sooo funny...*

Julo was still reading the open letter lying on the desk when he heard Erzsha enter the apartment. She came into the kitchen and realized that Julo had read Nora's letter.

"Why you are reading my letter?!" was her first sentence.

"I couldn't not read it," Julo's heart was still loudly pumping; he had to control himself.

"This is not what you think it is. Nora didn't understand what I wrote to her."

"And what did you write?"

"I was here alone. You were gone. I was horny. I went to clean Ted's apartment and that was it..."

"That was it? You were horny?" Julo couldn't believe what Erzsha was saying, "you don't have any better creep hole?"

"This was not a creep hole. This is what happened."

Julo didn't want to be there. He left the apartment, smashing the door behind him.

He went out and took a long walk. He couldn't control his anger. Her words came back into his mind. *She was horny and I should understand that? I can't believe she said that. I should understand her honest explanation of her affair and forgive? Ted is a prick. I knew he was...* By the time Julo had calmed down, he was on Charles Bridge. He pulled out the ring he bought in Slovakia and threw it into the Vltava River.

Passing moments 36 (1993).

Erzsha moved out of Julo's apartment the following week; Julo was glad he didn't have to tell her to do it. She moved back to Kosice and Julo felt relieved when she was gone. He went through all his pictures and shredded those showing Erzsha. On one hand Julo was now glad the relationship ended, on the other hand he was still upset and tried to understand what had happened.

So, you are in the relationship with somebody, you live with that person in one household for while; you are practically to married that person. You leave for two weeks, he or she gets horny. That is understandable in itself, humans are built that way, to get horny. Now you are that horny person, you need to release the pressure and you find an easy way to do that. Then your partner finds out about the way you released your pressure; you are an honest person and like to tell the truth so you tell it to your partner. It's his/her problem how he/she deals with that information; it's an honest, truthful explanation of the events but how are you, the guilty one, going to deal with your conscience? You go to the priest for confession, confess and are forgiven! Do I belong to this world? thought Julo.

Julo wanted to bury this part of his life deep, deep inside of him and hide it there untouched forever. He didn't go back to work for Ted Sekera. He decided to start his own business. He moved to a different apartment and bought a garage unit in which he could keep his construction tools. He had several friends who helped him with contacting potential customers, getting small remodeling projects. From the beginning he was doing mostly painting and simple remodeling projects. He didn't do any advertising. His customers spread the word about the quality of his work and from there new customers contacted him and his business started to pick up.

Passing moments 37 (1995).

It had been three years since Julo started his own construction business: Julo's Remodeling. He was now employing one full-time and one part-time helper. They did all types of home-improvement work including electrical, plumbing, brick laying and ceramic tile work. They could build a house from the foundation until the house was completely ready for the owner to move in. His precise, detailed work was paying off. He still didn't advertise. Some of his customers were willing to wait several months until Julo and his company were able to start working on their project.

Julo's personal life had changed too. He didn't practice AT anymore. There was no need for that; the depression that he had after his relationship with Lea ended was long-gone and there was no depression when Erzsha left; just relief. He still liked biking, playing tennis in the summer and skiing in the winter. In his free time he met his friends—mostly ex-coworkers from the construction company where he used to work when he first time moved to Prague—in the bowling club. It was there that he met Isabela, who was four years younger than Julo.

It was about 9:00pm Saturday night when Julo parked his car on the street about 50 yards away from the club. He stepped out from his car and noticed another car, a black Honda Civic that tried to back up and park in the empty space next to his car. He would go straight to the club but noticed that the Honda Civic couldn't maneuver into the available spot. Two girls stepped out of the car, started moving with their hands and talking to the driver.

"Isabela, turn wheel to the left, no, no, not that way to the left, another way to the left... stop, stop...hahaha" they were laughing while continuing to give Isabela further instructions "you need to go forward and try again."

Julo froze as the Honda Civic almost hit his new Volkswagen Jetta. Instead of going directly to the club he rather turned and walked back to his car.

"Hello ladies, can I help you somehow?" he asked the two girls standing outside on the street.

"Would you know how to get this car into that parking spot?" said the smaller, little bit bulkier girl.

"If you would trust me to do that I can certainly try" was Julo's reply.

"Yes, please. I simply don't know how to backup this car into that small place." That was Isabela's voice. She stepped out of the car and signed to Julo that the driving seat now waited for him. Isabela's curly dark hair and gentle smile attracted Julo's attention. He parked the Honda Civic right behind his Volkswagen Jetta, stepped out of the car and gave the key to Isabela.

"Thank you for your help," Isabela said, "You parked so easily. I am glad you came. I would almost certainly have scratched that car in front of mine."

"That is my car."

"Is it?" Isabela was laughing, "and you came here calmly without yelling at me? Tonight is my lucky day. I owe you a drink."

Passing moments 38 (1995-1996).

Isabela worked for a law firm as an office manager. She agreed to have a date with Julo, and then another, and another. Julo wanted to move the relation forward. He suggested to Isabela they go on a trip to the US west coast. Isabela turned out to be a trip planner. She bought the books about US places one should see and precisely planned the trip. They would land in Phoenix, Arizona, rent a car there, go south towards Tucson. They would visit Saguaro National Park first, then they would go to visit Old Tucson Studios.

"You will like that place, Julo, it was there where old west movies that you like so much, were shot."

After that they would go north towards Four Corners.

"Julo, that would be something; you would be in Arizona, make one step you are in New Mexico, third step you are in Colorado, fourth step and you are in Utah... hahahaha, you would visit four states within a minute; wouldn't that be wonderful! Before we get there we have to visit Petrified Forest National Park. We should see there lots of perhaps million years old wood that turned into stones! We would be inside of the Navajo and Apache Indian reservation. Like in those movies. We would go to their tents and smoke cigars of the peace."

After that they would go to Grand Canyon.

"We would not spend too much time there, Julo, we would just see this big hole and go towards Las Vegas. I would like to see also Lake Mead National Recreation Park before we get to Las Vegas. It is on the borders between Arizona and Nevada."

They would finish their trip in Las Vegas where they would return the rented car and fly back to Europe. Julo was amazed. It never got into his mind that the trip should be planned. At least not into the level of detail Isabela presented to him. He would just buy round trip airplane tickets to one of the US west coast cities, fly there and when he got there figure out what to do next.

Passing moments 39 (1996).

Isabela was sleeping in the passenger seat of the white Chevrolet Corvette newest 1996 model. Julo was driving the car through the Navajo Indian reservation. It was almost midnight, the road was straight. He realized that there had been no other car on the road for about an hour now. He looked at the tachometer. The maximum number on the tachometer watch was 180 mph. 180 miles per hour, that is about 290 kilometers per hour. Is that really how fast this car can go? Julo's leg pushed the gas pedal deeper. The tachometer speed watch went from 80, to 90 mph, then to 110, 120, 130. When it reached 140 mph the Chevrolet Corvette started to resonate. Julo had never driven a car at such speed as 220 kilometers per hour. He suddenly got scared. It looked to him that the car would fall apart. He released the gas pedal and let car slow down, back to 130, 120... when it was on 90 mph he noticed a light of the car coming from opposite direction. The lights of that car started to blink from strong to lower strength. Julo thought that the opposite car was blinking because the chauffeur of that car thought his head-light was on. Julo pushed his head-light switch several times to show to the opposite car coming towards him that he didn't have his head-lights on. The car was now almost next to him. *Gosh, this is a police car, not a regular driver signaling the strength of my lights. He was blinking to let me know that I am speeding.* The police car turned 180 degrees when it passed Julo's car and now instead of regular blinking Julo could see the blinking of the red/blue light color.

"Julo, you were speeding again!?" Isabela had woken woke up when Julo stopped their car and the policeman was approaching from the back.

"Just a little bit" Julo said and pulled his door window down.

"Good evening sir. Do you know why I stopped you?" the police officer asked Julo.

"Good evening sir. Yes I know. I was speeding."

"Do you know what your speed was?"

"Well, I didn't really paid attention. I know it was beyond the speed limit."

"Yes, it was almost 90 mph. Do you know that you are driving through a reservation? Do you know that there are cows and horses that could cross the road anytime? Can you imagine what could happen if you hit them with your speeding car?" The police officer was talking to Julo while examining his European driving license and his passport. "This time I will let you go without the ticket. But please slow down. The way you were driving was dangerous." The policeman gave back Julo his documents.

"Uf. I am lucky," said Julo to Isabela when they were back driving through the Navajo reservation. "Can you imagine that a policeman in our country would let me go without collecting a fine from me?"

"Julo, tell me what was your speed while I was sleeping?"

"Not much, just little bit over 100 mph…"

Passing moments 40 (1996).

"What a gorgeous view," Isabela said to Julo while looking at Colorado River carving through Grand Canyon. He had looked at Grand Canyon pictures before their trip; still to see this beautiful panorama picture in reality was an unexpected experience to him. It was the first week of spring; breeze in the air, sunny day with temperature about 50 degree Fahrenheit, snow still visible on the grass. They came there much sooner than Isabela's original plan schedule presumed.

"Julo, it's only 9:00am. Let's walk down on that hiking trail; we have plenty time to do quick hike down and then up."

"You mean down, down?" Julo was not sure what Isabela meant.

"Yeh, down, down. You see down there, it's camping area, we will get there and if we have time we can go all the way down to Colorado River."

"Isabela, please stop. This is not an easy, quick hiking trip. We were not planning to do this."

"You said that you never plan trips into the details. Don't be a milksop. We have tennis shoes; the weather is ideal, let's have a hike!"

Julo gave up and they both started to walk down the South Rim hiking trail towards the camping ground. They didn't have any bag, no food, not even a bottle of drinking water. Julo pointed to the 'DO NOT GO BEHIND THIS POINT IF YOU DON'T HAVE WATER' and tried for the last time to stop Isabela.

"Julo, we are almost half way, there is a drinking water down there in the camp. Another 20 minutes and we are there." She was correct. They were down at the camp ground quite quickly. It took them about 90 minutes to get from the parking lot where they left their rented car to have a drink of fresh water at the camping area.

"OK Isabela, but we are not going all the way down to Colorado River. It will take us two or three times longer to get back to our car." This time Isabela agreed and they started to walk back up around noon. The zig-zag hiking trail which was easy to walk down was not so easy on the way up. About one third of the way up Isabela sat on a stone and started to acknowledge her derogatory view of this hiking trip.

"OK, Isabela, we got down, we have to get up as well," Julo said with an encouraging voice. It was about 3pm when they made it halfway of their trip up. *Bad estimate, but not so bad,* Julo thought, *if we go on at this speed we should arrive around 6pm and eating a good dinner.* That was his only wish. Isabel sat on another stone and didn't want to continue.

"What do you mean I should go and you stay? You stand up and walk with me!" This time Isabel listened; she stood up and walked. In a much slower speed but she was walking. Three more hours took them halfway back and another three hours took them just to two-thirds of the way up. This time Isabela sat and didn't want to stand up and continue walking.

"No, Julo., you go I stay."

"Completely irrational statement. You really think that I would leave you here and continue walking by myself? Stand up and walk! Do you hear me?" She didn't. Julo had to sit with her for about 15-20 minutes and only after that Isabela could stand up and continue walking, or better say to be pulled by Julo, slowly up. It was 10:45pm when they got to the rest area where they could have a drink of fresh water.

Passing moments 41 (1996).

"Julo, Julo, can you hear me?"

"Yea, Isabela. It's only 10am. Why you are not sleeping?"

"I can't sleep anymore and I can't move. When I try to move it hurts, everywhere, each muscle hearts. Are you ok? Can you move?"

"I don't know. I haven't tried yet. I guess I can move. My muscles hurt too though."

"But you can move. Can you bring me breakfast?"

"I thought we would go together."

"But I can't move. I don't know what I am going to do. You are amazing, Julo. How you could you drive four hours from the Grand Canyon to here last night?"

"And where would we stay when we got up from Grand Canyon? It's because of your planning. If we didn't book a hotel in Las Vegas we could sleep somewhere near the Canyon."

"Sorry. Am I making your life hard?"

"No you don't. Yes you do! And wake up. I want to go for breakfast with you. My English is not as good. I wouldn't know how to order. I need you to go with me."

"You don't have to talk to them. Just put the food on the plate and bring it here. I told you, I can't move."

"It was your idea to hike the Grand Canyon without food and water! How could I be so stupid and listen to you?!" Julo's sentence didn't match his face. He was smiling at Isabela.

"Ha ha, stupid, stupid… You are glad that we went for that hike! Be honest, tell the truth… I can't move." Isabela tried slowly to wake up from the bed. She somehow did.

"You look like an old grandma that is going to be extinct very soon."

"Ha ha ha, very funny… Can you help me please?" Isabela leaned on Julo and he helped her to go to the bathroom. They managed to dress and go together for breakfast. Julo felt muscle pain as well. He could manage not to show it. Isabela was not able to do that. Her muscles hurt very much; she felt soreness in every square inch of her body.

They both felt better in the evening and could have a walk in Las Vegas's town square. Julo was amazed by so many hotels and casinos. They walked to one of them. Julo put several quarters in the slot machine and lost all of them. They bought drinks and watched other people play cards, poker and other gambling games. Isabela changed a ten dollar bill into quarters and started putting them into slot machine. Julo watched a poker gamer nearby. He turned his face towards one of the machines that was spitting out quarters. He saw Isabela's smiling face.

"You won?"

"Yes I did."

"How much?"

"Eighty dollars!"

"Oh wow, you are lucky. Can I have that money?"

"Yes, take them, what you are going to do with them?"

"Play a slot machine with dollar coins."

"…and you will lose all eighty dollars."

"If that happens it would be like we didn't win anything. Eighty dollars is not big win anyway." Julo started casting dollar coins one after another. No luck, no luck…

"Julo, stop, let's go away. I want to see other places. Let's go out of this casino." Isabela was on her way out.

"Trilililing, trilililing…" the slot machine stopped and started produce the winning jackpot melody.

"Isabela, we won again…" Julo announced loudly. Other people turned their eyes to have a look at the machine spitting large coins. "Guess how much?"

Isabela forgot about her muscle pain and wanted to run towards Julo. Her muscles didn't forget about yesterday's overload though; she had to slow down her rush towards Julo. Julo enjoyed her smiley face.

"Almost one of our airplane tickets has been fully paid by this machine," Julo announced as he hugged Isabela. "We won eight hundred dollars!"

They took the money and walked out of the casino.

Passing moments 42 (1996).

Two months after the overseas trip Julo suggested to Isabela that she move permanently into his apartment.

"Isabela, why are you paying for your shared room if most of the time you are here with me? Wouldn't make sense for you to just move here permanently?"

"Well, and if I do, wouldn't I become less precious for you?"

"Hm, I have never thought this could happen. I think I am looking at women differently now than I looked at them ten years ago."

"Differently? What do you mean?"

"I think I now appreciate different things more. For example I would like to have a partner that would for example do little bit of cooking and cleaning so when I get home I don't have to do this kind of work."

"Ha, forget it! You should find some Slovak girlfriend for that! Go ask Erzsha to move back to you! She was good cook! She kept your apartment clean!"

Julo was sorry now he told Isabela about Erzsha. "Ok, ok, stop, you don't have to remind me about my past relationships. You can go back to your boyfriend!"

"Which one?" There was little bit of an ironic smile on Isabela's face that Julo did not missed.

"You had more than one? You told me only about the one who had the BMW."

"I am teasing you… let's stop this quarrel, give me a kiss, here…" Isabela was pointing finger on her lips while pushing her head towards Julo. She knew Julo would not resist that; the fight stopped even before it really started.

Isabela moved into Julo's apartment the following week. It wasn't a big change for them. Isabela had most of her stuff already in Julo's apartment. What changed was Isabela's mailing address. Isabela wanted to pay her share of the rent. Julo convinced her instead of giving money to him to save it to pay her school. Isabela was planning to go back to school for her business administration BS degree.

There was a small change in their life after all. They were shopping more often together. Despite Isabela's claim she would not cook she started do some experimental cooking and she found out she liked it. She didn't clean the apartment regularly but didn't mind to put back stuff that Julo left behind him without reminding him she did that.

At the end of the same year they both agreed to marry each other. Neither wanted to go through a wedding ceremony. They had a small wedding reception with a few family members and close friends.

<u>Passing moments 43 (1997).</u>

Julo, 36, and Isabela, 32, had been married over a year. Isabela was pregnant. They agreed they would rather wait and be surprised by the gender of their babies, but they knew they would have twins. In the ninth month of Isabela's pregnancy the doctor scheduled the birth to be induced. Julo and Isabela went to the hospital on the morning of Friday April 21st 1997 and at 11 am Isabela gave birth to two girls.

Julo was in the room with Isabela, and so happy to see Kamilka born. Just a few moments later the doctor announced, "Here it comes, the second one!" Verunka was two minutes behind Kamilka and announced her entry to this world with a typical baby cry. Julo's mom insisted the girls must be baptized according to Catholic tradition, which Isabela was ok with, even though she herself was never baptized and wasn't part of any official religion and in fact considered herself an atheist. They could find a priest in Prague who would not follow strict Catholic rules and baptize both girls. In the eastern part of Slovakia most priests would insist that Isabela must be baptized as well and they would have had to be married in the church and only after that would the priest baptize girls as well. Julo knew that his mom would prefer that both of her daughters-in-law be baptized Catholic girls, but she liked Isabela despite her atheistic beliefs. Julo knew that his mom preferred Isabela's company to spending time with his younger brother's wife.

"Julo, just make sure the girls are baptized while I am still alive. They are God's creatures. He would take care of them if something happened to them; but they must be baptized." Julo's mother often said while he was on the phone to her.

The priest they found to do the baptizing ceremony offered a proposal that Julo and Isabela would take hourly catholic classes each week for about

6 month and after that he would baptize Isabela together with Kamilka and Verunka. He didn't insist that they should marry in the church too. Julo was surprised that Isabela agreed to this arrangement and looked forward to taking the classes. He knew she wouldn't change her atheistic belief, but he still liked her interest to learn more about Christianity and Catholic teaching. Julo liked classes as well. The classes he took when he was child came back to his mind. *What a difference*, he thought, *the teaching is now much more oriented towards historical fact than towards preaching how Catholics should leave and what rules should apply in his/her leaving.*

Passing moments 44 (1998).

Two weeks before Kamilka's and Verunka's first birthday celebration Julo's father passed away. He was 72-years-old when he died of a brain tumor. Julo anticipated his death as his father had been diagnosed with the disease at the beginning of the year. The grief that he felt was huge. In the nights when he tried to fall asleep memories of the moments that he spent with his father building the hen's shed came to mind; he couldn't resist the stream of tears.

He went to Slovakia for the funeral by himself, leaving Isabela, Kamilka and Verunka in Prague. It was a typical funeral for a small Slovak town: three short church bells announcing that somebody died 'bing…bing…bing' followed by massive bells ringing 'bing-bong-bang, bing-bong-bang…' A priest accompanied by a group of three ministrants holding crosses with portraits of Jesus followed by a casket with the dead body carried by six men, followed by the relatives and friends of the deceased walking towards the cemetery.

'*Remember, man, that dust you are and to dust you will return…*'

Moments of funerals stays in one's memory forever. The open casket laying on the stand in the funeral home so others can look at the dead body to give the last respects to a person who doesn't exist anymore. The shape of the dead body that has nothing to do with the shape of the same body that was occupied by the soul that ran this body several days ago; now the body is shrunk, become yellow and soon will turn into the dust. Memory remains.

Passing moments 45 (1998).

The day after his father's funeral Julo met up with his friends from University. They wanted to cheer Julo up; they talked about their time together in the dorm, remembering old friends, who was doing what.

"Have you heard what happened to Rose?" asked Vlado.

"Rose, you mean the girl from our dorm who was a year older than we were?" Julo asked.

"Yeah, the girl who wanted you badly and you were blind, deaf and dumb. She died in a car accident. You know that dangerous road twist near Sarisske Michalany? So many people had died there already. Her husband was driving fast, so the car went off the road and turned several times before landing on the roof. All of them dead; Rose, her husband and their two-year-old daughter."

Another blow hit Julo. The rain check issued by Rose to Julo had an expiration date after all.

There was another death. One of the boys that lived next door to his childhood home died too. Marko took his own life last year. He was the older son of two boys who attended the same middle and high school as Julo did. Their parents had finished building the house, moved in and right after that they divorced. Marko and his younger brother were in middle school and then lived with their mom only. Marko finished Technical University of Kosice, later got married and had one daughter.

Julo had met him several times when he visited his friends in Kosice. On those rare meetings Marko told Julo about his work problems, how his colleagues didn't understand why he created the computer software the way he did. Marko was unstoppable in his explanations. He explained his way of creating software to Julo and laughed at how his colleagues couldn't understand his software. Julo patiently listened, didn't understand his software either, neither understood why Marko was telling him about it at all, nor why Marko went into such detail. Did Marko think Julo would understand him? Did Marko inherit the same disease that Marko's father and grandfather had? The disease that the neighbor across the street described to his mom when he was a kid? What was the name of that disease? Schizophrenia, no, no his neighbor had different name for it: schoziforia.

Passing moments 46 (1998).

The same day Julo came back home from Slovakia, the week before Kamilka's and Verunka's birthday, Julo witnessed Kamilka's first steps. Verunka took completely different approach to her steps than Kamilka did. Verunka slowly, day by day, stood up next to the sofa or bed or anything to which she could put her hand, then slowly move next to that sofa, then try to take hand away from the sofa just for the couple seconds to see whether she could stand by herself and rather put her hand right back on the sofa than take a risk of falling down.

Kamilka simply decided that she would start walking in that particular second; she stood up next to the sofa with a big smile on her face and started to walk towards the middle of the room, then stopped for a while and continued walking as if this was nothing new for her. Verunka started to walk about same time as Kamilka did; but it was not a sharp cut between walking with help and walking completely without any hesitation. It's was like the difference between analog and digital signal processing. In analog the signal goes continuously up, gets to its peak and then continuously down, another peak, then continuously up. Digital signal knows only zeros or ones, creates the sequence of information by jumping from one peak (=zero), remains on that peak for certain time period and changes to another peak (=one).

Passing moments 47 (1999).

"Kamilka and Verunka are 18-months-old, we should start to train them to sleep by themselves now. I read in the book that they should be left in the bedroom alone, parents should resist coming back when they start crying, after a while they will stop crying and eventually fall to sleep without mama or daddy next to them," Isabela said one evening to Julo.

They both agreed to try this approach. They put them in their own cots, gave them kisses and closed the door. Kamilka realized that this was a plot and displayed her temper in full beauty. She started loudly crying first, then since parents would not come to their bedroom she grabbed the bars on the cot and with much louder crying tried to push her body over the top of the bar constraint. Verunka was sitting on the bed and was crying but with not such resistant power as Kamilka was.

Julo and Isabela were sitting on the living room sofa. The time was going slowly for them. They thought that the girls cried for at least two hours and they decided to give up. In reality, the crying had been going on for about 15 minutes when they entered girls' bedroom. Julo took Kamilka and Isabela, Verunka into their arms and tried to calm them down.

"Who wrote that stupid advice encouraging parents to just close the kid's door and then resist their crying?" Julo blamed solely Isabela for trying to implement this idea even though he fully agreed to participate in it. No, in his mind this experiment had nothing to do with him, the blame belonged to somebody else.

Passing moments 48 (2002).

It was Isabela who took a responsibility to make sure that both kids learnt what they should learn at their particular age. She signed up the kids for swimming lessons in the summer when they were three years old and to skating lessons in the winter when they were one year older. She signed them up for children's ballet classes, step dance classes, gymnastic classes. Some of the classes the kids enjoyed, some of them they resisted to take. Julo liked the way Isabela took charge of this. He would not mind buying some cheaper bikes just so the kids could have one. It was Isabela who easily convinced him to purchase better more expensive bikes for both of them. He was glad Isabela was there to take good care of their children.

Passing moments 49 (2003).

Julo and Isabela bought a new four-bedroom condominium. Before they moved in Julo and his company did the remodeling work, designed by Isabela. They looked forward to moving into a new condo. Their six-year-old twins would have their own rooms and they wouldn't have to be crowded into their small apartment anymore. Julo's construction company was doing well and he was earning decent money. Isabela had a good steady income working for the law firm. They could afford to spend two weeks of vacation each summer in sea resorts, and in the winter to ski in the Alps for seven days. All was looking good except that Isabela was not really happy with the type of work Julo was doing.

"Julo, you have a master's degree in physics, you have four years of experience in computers and robotics, and you are just a simple construction worker," Isabela's words bothered Julo. He was not sure whether he would be able to catch up with the science field or get back to computer type of work. It was true that he didn't like dealing with his customers, and he hated doing taxes and all the bureaucratic work connected with his business. Julo, now 42, started to think about whether he was satisfied with the work that he was doing, with the life that he was living. He compared himself with his university fellows and thinking about who was doing what now, he found he was not satisfied with his life achievements.

The time he spent with Lea came back to his mind; she hadn't disappeared from his memory. Julo didn't remember the moment when her image came back to his inner life but when it did his relatively calm and enjoyable life took a different turn. His memory brought up the events from over 20 years ago and as he reflected on them he found himself reacting angrily. He was a fool; he did everything to please her. For three years he tried to show Lea his best; writing poems, bringing small gift surprises, he even tried to learn to play the guitar (what a stupid, foolish thing to do – he never could be a guitar player). He did all this to fulfill his build-in reproduction gene-print; the reward that should have belonged to him was awarded to somebody else. Thus Lea's image became the object of Julo's inner anger. He internally blamed her for his misspent youth. *She got me; how could I be so stupid? How did I let myself be sucked into her imaginary love world and behave according to her rules, only to be kicked off when she became bored by me.'* These thoughts became more and more massive, and created a scalding base for Julo's inner volcano of anger.

Passing moments 50 (2004).

Julo's inner world of anger started to affect his behavior. He repeated to himself the past events that happened decades ago. In his inner thinking he convinced himself that his youth was misspent and there was somebody else that he blamed for that. This pathological way of thinking hidden inside of him started to take a toll. He was losing his patience more often than he should, and started to yell at his children for their small misbehaviors.

"Julo, you are yelling and raising your voice without any reason," Isabela told him several times. Julo was convinced that his reactions were reasonable and justified. He now had inside of him the same anger he loathed so much when he was young boy; and worse, he started to throw that anger at others in a similar way to how it was thrown at him by his father when he was a kid. At that time he was the sensitive recipient of the anger; now he didn't comprehend that he was the owner of that anger and he was throwing his anger unexpectedly at others.

His mind worked differently now. During the night before he fell asleep he couldn't hear the noise of his heart and wonder what it was, like he did when he was young boy; he couldn't create images like he did when he as a kid thinking of which girl he would take into his future car. His cognitive thinking was freezing, not creating images that would make him happy.

Passing moments 51 (2004).

Julo's wife, Isabela, had been diagnosed with leukemia cancer in October 2004. The doctors' prognosis was that she had no more than 10 months to live and they were correct. After ten months of going to doctor visits, fighting hospital bureaucracy, watching Isabela losing her faith, the ordeal was now over when Isabela passed away. She died at home in the late morning hours. Kamilka and Verunka were with grandparents.

Julo had taken off the entire week from work to be home with Isabela. She was lying in the bed still alive when he came to see her shortly before 11am. She asked Julo to give her his hand. When he did so she looked at him with pain in her eyes, tried to smile, then closed her eyes, forever... Julo froze. He knew this moment would come. He was preparing himself; he thought he was... now when that moment arrived he didn't know what to do; he was frozen, holding Isabela's hand... The scene from his childhood when he visited Krskova's house to see Gitka's dead body surfaced from the depth of his mind. Suddenly he understood Gitka's father Anthony's pain and his cry that he witnessed 34 years ago. He did the same thing now as he did: put his palms around Isabela's face, put his cheek on Isabel's cheek, his tears were running down from his eyes when he whispered to Isabela's right ear: "Wake-up, Isabela, wake-up... please wake-up, wake-up..."

Passing moments 52 (2005).

Family life with Isabela was over. Julo had been now coping with a different type of day-to-day reality. Kamilka and Verunka went through children's psychological therapy, but Julo insisted he didn't need any. Julo's parents-in-law, Isabela's parents, were a big help. They took Kamilka and Verunka to their house as much as Julo allowed them to do so. Julo started blaming himself for not making Isabela's life more enjoyable; he didn't try well enough to be a better husband, he raised his voice to her so many times.

Julo now hated his life. His life looked normal to others. Kamilka and Verunka were in the second grade in elementary school and they stayed in the afterschool program. Julo usually picked them up around 5:00pm, parking his car on Plzenska Street right around the corner from the elementary school. One afternoon after he picked up the kids he came back to his car to find it was not there. At first he thought he parked illegally and that his car was towed away. He called the towing company; they told him that they didn't tow any car from Plzenska Street today. Julo then called police department to report that his car was stolen.

"Are you sure, sir, that you parked car on Plzenska Street?" asked the officer on the other end of the telephone line.

"Yes, I am sure. I always park my car on Plzenska Street when I pick up my children," Julo answered.

"Can you please tell me what day today is?" asked the officer.

"What kind of questions are you giving me?" Julo's voice was getting angry.

"Answer the question please."

Julo realized that he was not sure whether it was Wednesday or Thursday.

"Who cares what is the day today. Somebody has stolen my car, I need help!"

"Sir, do not yell into the phone please."

Julo smashed the phone down. Little blonde Kamilka and Verunka watched their dad, not understanding why dad got so angry. Julo suddenly realized that he didn't park his car on Plzenska Street. There was no parking spot on Plzenska so he parked his car on the next street he found an empty spot. He walked with Kamilka and Verunka to the street around the corner from Plzenska Street and there was his car! He and his daughters got into his car and went home, not believing what just happened to him.

He had completely lost his memory, didn't remember the events, where he parked his car, that he had left the car on a completely different street. This was not the first time that he noticed that he was losing his memory, that he had a hard time remembering what happened just several minutes ago.

Passing moments 53 (2006).

Julo first met Kristina at the party that Isabela's law office gave several years ago. He knew Kristina was divorced and didn't have any children. He also knew that she got married when she was very young, still a teenager, and her marriage lasted less than a year. The gossip about her story was that she got pregnant when she was seventeen, married a sweetheart she was dating at that time then shortly after the wedding she miscarried and then after several months divorced. She was more than 20 years younger than Julo.

Julo invited Kristina for a movie, then the next week for a dinner date. Kamilka and Verunka liked Kristina and Kristina liked them. Kristina liked to talk and had her comments on everything. Perhaps because of her first marriage experience she had decided to have sex only after she was married. Julo didn't like that but didn't raise an objection either. He wondered whether there was something within him that attracted women that don't want to have sex (at least not with him) right after he meets them. Did he present himself as morally solid person, women liked that and therefore wanted to match that morality? He laughed to himself at that explanation.

After several months of dating Kristina moved to live with Julo and his two daughters. On the weekends Julo usually woke up earlier and went to buy doughnuts for his girls. He had to buy two more now since it turned out that Kristina liked the doughnuts too. Kristina was rather slim with dark, wavy hair; a nice looking woman. Eating doughnuts for her breakfast took a toll. She started gaining weight, mainly around the waist. One afternoon after examining her body in the mirror she said to Julo, "Julo look…" she pointed to her stomach, "look, I think I am pregnant."

Julo's first thought was that she was joking.

"Yeah, got pregnant, the same way as the Virgin Mary, by saint spirit."

"I don't understand your way of joking. I must be pregnant, look at my stomach."

"Yep, it is getting bigger by eating doughnuts."

"You are buying those things so I am eating them. I can eat what I want and don't gain weight by that!"

"I am just wondering how the sperm could get there. I obey the rule you set it up," Julo smiled at Kristina.

"You don't really obey it. I don't want to be pregnant yet. I don't know how exactly but I think I am pregnant."

Julo started to wonder whether Kristina knew exactly how human bodies worked. At the same time he was thinking whether there could be a way sperm would get there without intercourse. What a silly thought. It turned out that Julo's theory as to why Kristina's waist increased in its size was correct. Julo was not sure whether Kristina was disappointed that she was not pregnant after all; shortly after that she gave up her pledge of not having sex before marriage.

Passing moments 55 (2007).

Julo and Kristina married at the end of 2007. They had small wedding ceremony with close friends and a few relatives.

"You are nice looking couple; beautiful young bride; not so young but still handsome groom. Listen, tell me, what I am doing wrong? Why I don't attract young, beautiful girls as you do?" his cousin Stanley asked him when they were outside of the restaurant during the wedding reception and continued without waiting to get an answer, "you were always lucky at attracting pretty girls; hey, what happened to your first one? What was her name? Yeah, Lea, what happened to her?"

Julo noticed that his heart started to pound when he heard Lea's name.

"I don't know. I haven't seen her since I was… I don't even remember how old I was when I last time saw you," Julo tried to say this in as easy and calm voice as he could, he didn't want to Stanley to see how his inner world reacted just from hearing Lea's name.

Julo was glad he got married to Kristina. He wanted to have somebody next to him. On the other hand, he was not able to manage his inner thoughts. Just by hearing Lea's name the thoughts about her betrayal started pounding his mind. The thoughts about Lea that surfaced before Isabela's diagnosis were suppressed by life events only for a short time period. The scalding volcano of his anger had not disappeared and his thoughts of how he was betrayed more than twenty years ago were waiting to surface again, his self-pitying thoughts came back to him as well; now amplified by the guilt of Isabela's death. Unstoppable blaming: blaming himself for not providing to Isabela what he thought he could; blaming somebody else for something that happened so many years ago.

Julo created a fighting zone inside of him. He created the answers to the questions that could be potentially asked while talking to a person he thought he would talk to soon. *Why am I creating these scenarios? They in reality never go the way I imagine them to go?* Julo thought to himself. But he couldn't stop creating the dramatic performances in the theater of his mind. He noticed that instead of regular thinking his thoughts were often automatically converted to inner dialogue, as if he was talking or explaining to somebody in particular an imaginary situation. The thoughts would just come. The most common stage performance involved imaginary questions and answers to Lea; creating a stage in which he would tell her, in the smartest, wittiest way, what she had done to him.

Julo's inner battles were hardly noticeable by the outside world. Referring to Kamilka, asking her what she was doing while facing Verunka, was nothing uncommon for a parent of twins. But it was worse than that. Julo was now forgetting the names of his friends and he couldn't always retrieve the correct word to name an object. He started hesitating about which way to go when he was driving home on the roads that he had taken dozens of times. The words *I hate this life* began repeating in his brain over and over again.

Passing moments 56 (2008).

Julo, Kristina, Kamilka and Verunka were going for their first summer vacation to the Canary Islands. Julo bought a book about the Canary Islands and gave it to Kristina expecting her to plan everything the same way Isabela did.

"Why did you buy this book?" Kristina asked Julo when she saw the book.

"I thought you would like that." Julo realized Kristina is not Isabela and was disappointed they didn't plan their vacation the same way as he did with Isabela.

They took Czech Airlines to Santa Cruz, the capital of the islands, rented a car there and planned to spend most of their vacation on the archipelago's beaches.

Julo's sense of orientation started to deteriorate. He was afraid that he would not be able to drive from their bungalow to the beaches; that he would get lost. He drove rather slowly, and always asked Kristina which way they should go. When they visited Teide National Park, he asked Kristina to drive. He preferred not to go to too many places and instead stayed on the beach most of the time.

He was glad when the vacation was over and their airplane landed back in Prague. They decided to take a subway back to their apartment. Suddenly Julo felt lost and couldn't figure out where he needed to insert his subway ticket.

"I am starting to be scared of you, Julo, here, the ticket needs to go here," said his wife Kristina as she showed him where to put his ticket.

Julo tried to make light of this event, "Oo, gosh, I need to pay better attention so I know where I am," he smiled at Kristina.

Passing moments 57 (2008).

Julo attended the funeral of his dearest friend's mom. He always liked to spend time with her when he visited his friend Jozef in Slovakia. He first met Jozef in Hradec Kralove when he was serving for the military in the old regime. They didn't see each other very often; however they both felt good when they saw each other again.

82

Julo enjoyed listening to the words of the priest during the funeral mass ceremony. They were words of wisdom read from the Old Testament Ecclesiastes 3;1-8:

> *There is a time for everything,*
> *and a season for every activity under the heavens:*
> *a time to be born and a time to die,*
> *a time to plant and a time to uproot,*
> *a time to kill and a time to heal,*
> *a time to tear down and a time to build,*
> *a time to weep and a time to laugh,*
> *a time to mourn and a time to dance,*
> *a time to scatter stones and a time to gather them,*
> *a time to embrace and a time to refrain from embracing,*
> *a time to search and a time to give up,*
> *a time to keep and a time to throw away,*
> *a time to tear and a time to mend,*
> *a time to be silent and a time to speak,*
> *a time to love and a time to hate,*
> *a time for war and a time for peace.*

There was so much truth in those words. He thought of his daughters. He was not raising them as his mom had raised him and his brother, insisting that they go to church every Sunday. *It's not too late*, he thinks, *I should start to take them to church so the words the priest is repeating will stick in them too.* His thoughts were re-enforced with the next sentence coming from the priest, repeating Jesus's words in John 14:27.

"*Peace I leave with you; my peace I give you. I do not give you as the world gives. Do not let your hearts be troubled and do not be afraid.*"

Julo knew there was no peace inside of him.

Passing moments 58 (2009).

Julo went to the Hornbach home improvement store where he purchased three fine finished pine boards. He needed the boards for the project on which he was working. He paid for the boards and only afterwards, when he was loading the boards into his van, did he realize that one board was damaged. He thought that since he just purchased the boards it should be an easy process to swap the damaged board with a good one without going through the return station at another end of the store. He thought he would go in through the exit; he would show an exit guard the damaged wood and replace that wood with a good one without any hassle.

When he entered the store via the exit door he explained to the store-guard, a lady in her sixties, what he would like to accomplish. The lady understood Julo's intent but didn't want to bend Hornbach's store rules.

"Yes, sir. I understand what happened. You will have to go to the return-store counter and explain to them what happened. They will help you with that.

"So, for this simple board replacement you want me to go to another end of the store, wait there thirty minutes until I get a chance to explain that I was not paying attention when I took and paid for this damaged piece of wood, that I took from the store aisle right behind you not more than ten minutes ago?!" Julo couldn't control his anger made obvious in his voice that was louder than it should be.

"Sir, those are the store rules, once you have paid for the item it can be exchanged only through the return department."

"So, you don't have your own thinking?! You can't make your own reasonable decision? Make an exception that makes sense and simply let me put this damaged piece of wood in the row behind you and take instead wood that is not damaged!?" Perhaps if Julo did not raise his angry voice and rather tried to convince the guard in a nice way, perhaps he would achieve his objective. He was not capable of doing that, not in his current state of mind. He didn't shout but continued with anger in his voice. "...Instead you prefer to make the shopping in this store miserable, you decided to be a person that always behave by the rules and you are going to force everybody including me in this very moment to obey those stupid rules!"

After that as Julo turned away from the guard towards the exit door he noticed the tears in her eyes which turned into crying as she went in the opposite direction away from him.

He got to his van with the same damaged pine board, still angry, repeating in his mind what he just said to the guard, trying to convince himself that he reacted in the correct way and at the same time putting together different sentences which he thought he could have used in the moment that passed couple minutes ago. Even when driving his van his mind still repeated and created variations on sentences that could have been said in this short life interaction between two people.

The tears that he saw in lady's eyes made him uncomfortable; he reminded himself *I hate this life.*

Passing moments 59 (2009).

In Julo's new kind of everyday inner life he often repeated the same words to himself: *I hate this life. I hate the buzz in my head. I hate, I hate, I hate.* Talking to himself he created stages inside of his mind in which he came up with the best answers to imaginary situations.

The buzzing inside of his brain that had started several years ago and was at first hardly noticeable, changed now to a higher pitch frequency and got louder. Julo learned not to be bothered with this constant buzz; what started to be annoying was the buzz mixed with the fogginess inside of his brain. It was in those moments that Julo couldn't think clearly. Those moments sometimes lasted a couple of minutes, sometimes a couple of hours.

His memory was getting worse and worse. He started to be surprised by something that he himself created. For example he read the sentences that he knew he wrote but it looked to him like he was reading them for the first time; he didn't remember when he himself had done it. His brain stopped to put together his own passing moments and stopped creating from those moments the meaningful image called life. He felt like he was falling into a black hole in which there was no life that he remembered he lived as a child. He walked on the streets that should have been familiar to him, as he had been walking them for the past several years, but he was lost now and glad when he could somehow get home.

He tried to remember simple things that happened a few minutes ago but he couldn't; it was hard for him to read a page and understand what he just read. How long could he go on like that? His brain was completely falling apart; his cognitive thinking was no longer cognitive.

He went on like that for several months with it getting worse and worse; he sometimes couldn't even remember the words to put together a coherent sentence. He knew it was bad, he knew the outside world didn't see his inside troubles and he didn't want to reveal them.

He was sitting behind the kitchen table in his fifth-floor apartment looking at the window confused, not sure where he was, what day it was, who was around him. Then suddenly he knew what he would do; he was going to open the kitchen window...

Chapter 4: Put the Sky Inside of You

Event Horizon

Jirka's mind went back to Julo's funeral, which had shaken him deeply. He wondered whether there had been a way to prevent what happened to Julo. Seeing Kamilka and Verunka at the funeral was one of the most heartbreaking things he had ever experienced. And Jozef was not there. Why didn't he show up? They were good friends during their Hradec Kralove time. *He must have had a reason for not coming,* he thought. *I would like to see him again, tell him what has happened to me since our time together in Hradec Kralove. How many years is it? 25 or 26?* Jirka's thoughts continued. *The priest at Julo's funeral had a point when he said that it would be too easy to say 'How he could do that?!' How he could be so selfish and leave his two kids behind? We don't know why! We don't know the exact reason. We don't know what was going on inside of his head.*

Jirka's mind wandered back to Hradec Kralove when he and Jozef debated about IQ. Jirka liked those debates. He considered Jozef a walking Wikipedia. He remembered their debates about the universe, stars, black holes, how hard it was to understand how the black holes happen. Jozef words popped-up in his mind: "If you got to that black hole the way time and space behave is completely un-imaginable; for example you could meet there with yourself." Jirka remembered how he was smiling, couldn't imagine how this could happen but liked to listen Jozef's lectures.

The black hole theory since their Hradec Kralove time had advanced rapidly. Today astronomers consider the black holes as one of the easiest of universe's occurrences to explain. The easy way to remember how the black hole happens is to imagine that the mass collapses into itself; in order to do that the mass needs to be very big, at least three times bigger than mass of Sun. The black hole has its core which is somewhere in the middle; around the black hole's core is the singularity layer followed by an inner layer, going towards the mouth of the black hole is an outer layer.

26 years after the black hole debate in Hradec Kralove, Jirka now got curious and started to search for the answer, but was not able to find any article about the possibility of meeting yourself inside of the black hole. Was the stuff he discussed with Jozef decades ago pure sci-fi or was there some scientific base? While searching through black hole theories Jirka found some interesting stuff called the event horizon theory. Event horizon: the area right where the mouth of black hole eats whatever comes to that point; once any mass gets through the event horizon it can't send any information out of the black hole. Things get even more interesting when classical mechanics of physics and quantum mechanics try to explain whether any particle can ever escape out of the black hole. Classical mechanics claimed nothing could escape out of the black hole in the same way that the sun would rise tomorrow morning.

Quantum mechanics was more fun. They played with the words and would rather claim that the sun would most likely rise tomorrow morning but there was an almost negligible probability that it would not. In a similar way, quantum mechanics explained the possibility of events on the event horizon: for every particle there is antiparticle, both with the same mass but opposite electric charge and they can annihilate each other when they get close together. If this pair of particle-antiparticle is created just right behind the event horizon, quantum mechanics says that there is a possibility that one part could be drawn inside of the black hole while other is ejected out. The part that is ejected would quickly steal and take out some extra energy from that black hole; that stealing would cause the decay of black hole and for the next particle-antiparticle pair it would be little bit easier to repeat what the first pair have done, then the chain reaction would continue until the black hole disappeared.

Could it be that the human brain has its own black hole? Jirka pondered. When cognitive thinking is getting closer to it's own event horizon outsiders observe this as a debilitating stage of disease: Alzheimer's, Dementia, Multiple Sclerosis, Schizophrenia, etc. The insider who is moving towards the black hole, but still far away from the event horizon, first notices only small changes in their cognitive system functionality: typical human things such forgetting names, forgetting where things were put, small confusion of place or bad space orientation.

The insider knows that he is getting closer to the event horizon when he doesn't remember who is who, can't put sentences together, he is lost in places, his brain is constantly creating imaginary situations which prohibit him from thinking clearly. Then human thinking passes the boundary of the black hole's event horizon and there is no way that any information from the insider's cognitive thinking can get out to the outside world. *Was Nietzsche in that stage at the end of his life?* Jirka wondered.

The insider knows he is there, he knows his cognitive system is dispersing within the black hole and he is not able to send information to the outside world; to let that world know what is happening to his cognitive thinking. Here it comes: according to the theory of quantum mechanics then; cognitive thinking might not be gone forever. There might be those special circumstances when particle-antiparticle of cognitive thinking gets behind the event horizon and one is drawn inside of the black hole while other is ejected out with this extra energy taken out of the black hole!

Am I that lucky man? Jirka asked himself, *I know I was behind my event horizon. Am I far away from the outer layer?* Jirka was not convinced yet that this was the case.

Jirka thought for a long time about putting his own experiences on paper. What would he have advised Julo to do if he had a chance to talk to him soon enough, before Julo opened that window? Jirka remembered that Julo read all Levi's books. Jirka would not have to work on convincing Julo about the power that the human brain possesses.

Julo mastered his AT relaxation techniques very well already in his twenties; he demonstrated that during our time in Hradec Kralove. There was something somewhere that Julo either missed or had not done the correct way. I bet Julo knew he had to do something with his inner life in his twenties. Why otherwise would he read all Levi's books? It was not just reading the book for the sake of reading, Jirko thought. *How does one know when he needs to work on his own lifestyle and change it? How does one know that the way he thinks will take him to the event horizon? He wouldn't know, wouldn't care, until he hits that zone. When he does that, it might be too late. Not everybody is lucky enough to open Levi's books, Yalom's books, Amen's books, soon enough for his cognitive thinking to still be capable of comprehending the situations, understand the advice found in those books and get out of the event horizon before the black hole takes him completely in.*

Julo started, practiced good stuff for a while and then stopped, Jirko thought, *there is no end point on the things that work; they should become lifetime habits. It's not like I can start exercise, do my meditation for a certain time period until I achieve my goals and after that I don't have to do anything, time freezes, and 'heaven on earth' comes and I will enjoy that frozen moment of happiness until the end of time. This doesn't exist, of course not; what exists is creating the correct lifestyle and sticking to it as the way I live my life; stick to it and never stop!*

If you want to do that, change your lifestyle, you need to know yourself. Here comes the very tricky part, Jirko thought: *You can't know yourself if you don't change, really change, everything that is inside of you. So it's like a puzzling looping circle: where to start? The answer could be: Start with putting the sky inside of you, yes, "Put the sky inside of you."*

Why the sky? Why not for example music? To put music inside of my mind would be horrible Jirka thought. *I hear some song and then that song is there, repeating itself in my brain, sometimes it is hard to stop that repeating, that would not be a good choice, it would be a horrible choice. OK, no music so why not then for example a meadow? Yeh, that could be interesting to do as well. Still, I'd rather stick to putting the sky inside of me!*

Jirka grabbed this thought like a drowning person grabs anything that is near him to rescue himself. He created his own 30-minute stretching/ yoga sequence and decided to practice it regularly every day, once at the start of the day, and once in the afternoon. On top of that he did AT from time to time too.

Jirka practiced a series of yoga postures with focus on slow breaths that stretched his body and calmed his mind. During each position Jirka looked at the sky; at the end he placed his palms over his eyes and opened them while breathing in and out slowly – it was then he would try to remember the sky image.

Simple meditation practices; was not that what he used to do when he was a kid? He did exactly this: placed palms over his eyes to see what dark looks like and he was amazed by how little of the light that he could see.

No matter how hard he tried to close the gaps on his palms he still would see little bit of light.

During the day, whenever he could, he looked at the sky and tried to keep the image in his memory. The sky didn't want to get in so easily; his mind was too close to the event horizon. To begin from that point to re-train the cognitive system was not an easy task. But he knew he must do something and must stick to it. Nietzsche's attitude helped him: "That which doesn't kill us, makes us stronger."

Aunt Gertruda

Jirka grew up in the small village near Prague. His family's house was divided similar to many townhouses: into two parts; old and very old. He, his two older brothers and his parents lived in the old house. Aunt Gertruda lived in very old part of the house, built sometime in the 19th century. Both rooms of this very old house had an earthen floor. The entry room was a kitchen where Aunt Gertruda from time to time cooked something on the fire-stove. She knew that Jirka and his brothers would come once they smelt the food so she always cooked more; enough for everybody. She would feed them as if they were her own children. The second room was the living room and at the same time the bedroom. Gertruda put a hand-made carpet on the floor so the room would look cozier.

Jirka's older brother by three years, Ludvig, often slept in Gertruda's house when he became teenager. The old part of the house was locked when he came home late after midnight during his weekends hangouts with his friends; rather than knock on the door of the old house he knocked on Aunt Gertruda's door. He would hear Gertruda coming to the door asking, "Who is there?"

"It's me, Gertruda, open the door..." Ludvig knew she wouldn't mind being woken up and would let Ludvig in without any preaching that was too late and asking questions where he was and why he is not going to sleep in his own bed.

Gertruda never married, didn't have her own children, and Jirka never found out whether she had ever dated anyone. He heard stories from other people in the neighborhood that during World War 2 the Germans took Gertruda with other young women to Germany for forced work. Gertruda worked in a sewing factory with other Czech, Polish, and Slovak women. The story was that one day during the transportation from one factory to another the train was hit with a bomb which killed several women. Gertruda survived but was mentally affected since then. When Jirka asked Gertruda to tell him about her time in Germany she just told him a few sentences in German and didn't go into any details.

Jirka together with Ludvig often quietly went to the kitchen of Gertruda's home and listened to Gertruda's self talking: "And why did she come here to borrow the scissors from me? Why she didn't go to her sister! She came and said 'Gertruda, do you have scissors? I can't find mine.' She didn't try to find them; she came directly to me to take mine! And now I don't have scissors…" This was (at least for Jirka) like secretly watching an actor performing on the stage. Gertruda changed her voice when she was repeating what the neighbor told her when she came to borrow the scissors. Gertruda didn't know that somebody else was observing her self-talk.

Ludvig disrupted Gertruda's self talk and entered the living room: "Gertruda, why didn't you say to the neighbor that you would not loan your scissors! Now you are upset about that and talking to yourself like crazy person!" Gertruda, within a tenth of the second, realized that she was overheard, didn't make any big deal out of it and simply answered to Ludvig "and why didn't she go to her sister to borrow the scissors?!"

"Gertruda, you don't understand! I am telling you, you should tell her that when she was here! Not tell it to yourself when she is gone!" Ludvig raised his voice, almost yelling at Gertruda what she should do when her visitor came to her house. Gertruda, instead of getting on Ludvig, telling him that a thirteen-year-old boy should talk differently to his aunt, just quietly acknowledged her guilt.

"Yes, yes I should…"

Ludvig and Jirka knew she wouldn't do that. Gertruda didn't know how to say, "No I will not go to the store to buy groceries for you, I am not your slave; no I will not loan my scissors to you, I know you will not return them unless I remind you several times to do so; no you go and knock on the next house door so your father knows what time you came home…" She wasn't capable of saying that; instead without any resistance she did what she had been asked to do or give what she was asked to give up. She knew that other people were taking an advantage of her; perhaps that was the reason she created an imaginary person to whom she loudly told what happened to her.

Gertruda managed to live with her self-talking life with decent normality until her late fifties. When Jirka came back from Hradec Kralove he noticed that Gertruda had changed. She now more often asked Jirka for some pain-killers, "Jirka would you get me something for the pain?"

"What kind of pills you would like to get?"

"I don't know, something that kills the pain."

"And where do you feel pain Gertruda?"

"Everywhere Jirka; would you get some pills against headache?"

Gertruda would use any pills that Jirka or whoever else would bring to her and tell her were good to kill the pain.

Two years later when Jirka was about twenty-five years old he asked Gertruda to go with him to the County office. Jirka's parents would like to make some changes; they suggested to Jirka that he should take down the very old house and build a new house there. They thought that Jirka and Margareta would live there when they got married. In order to do that, Gertruda as a house co-owner, had to sign a document. Jirka explained to Gertruda why they had to go to County office.

"Yes Jirka, yes I will do what you want me to do," Gertruda told Jirka.

"Gertruda, you understand why we have to go to that office, right? You understand that they will ask you to sign a document confirming that the ownership of this old house will be transferred to me?" Jirka explained to Gertruda for the third time the reason for their trip to the County office.

"And where I will be living if you take my house away from me?" she asked.

Jirka felt bad when he heard that question.

"Gertruda, we will build a new house. During the construction you will be living in my room. After new house is built you will have your own new room, you will have your own bathroom."

"My own bathroom? And will you take me to a spa resort? I would like to go to the spa." Going to a spa resort was Gertruda's dream. She thought that the bath in the warm spa water would have a miracle affect on her.

"Yes, Gertruda, I will take you to the spa. But do you understand why we will go to County office tomorrow and what the officer might ask you?"

"I don't know, Jirka. What they will ask me?

"Gertruda, I told you that already." Jirko was not giving up and patiently explained to Gertruda the reason why they had to go to the County office. Jirka understood that Gertruda had been losing touch with reality. Still he took Gertruda into his car the next morning and went to the office to meet an attorney that would observe the signature procedures and confirm the transferral of the house ownership. The attorney was an older sister of his friend.

She started ask questions.

"Mrs. Gertruda, do you know why we are here today?"

After a moment of silence Gertruda replied, "Jirka asked me to come here with him."

"Do you understand my question?" The attorney now realized that Gertruda didn't fully understand where she was. "Do you understand where you are?"

Gertruda didn't understand where she was. Her inner life took her away from the life of the other people who were surrounding her

"Mrs. Gertruda, do you know what day it is today?"

Jirka and the attorney observed Gertruda's foggy look. She didn't know what day it was. Her inner life didn't pay attention to how days went by.

"I am sorry, we can't do the ownership transaction with Gertruda. Somebody would have to obtain the power of attorney that would authorize him or her to act as Gertruda's guarantor," the attorney told Jirka and as she followed them to the exit door.

Jirka in his forties

Jirka tried hard. He worked on putting the sky inside of him no matter what, no matter how long it took. The sky was not in yet; what he felt was that his "I" started coming up from a deep hole within him. Jirka felt he needed more than regular everyday AT practice or everyday yoga focus. He didn't know yet what else he needed exactly, he just knew he needed to get more wisdom to deal with himself.

Where else would a person look for wisdom if not in books? Jirka was not a reading maniac. He liked to ready only certain types of books. The books that attracted him the most were the ones where he could find himself. For example, a book by Irvin Yalom "The Schopenhauer Cure".

Jirka could find himself almost in every person of the therapy group described in that particular book. He, like Phillip, was obsessed with sex. The main difference was that Jirka didn't try to have sex with as many women as he could, that was not his case, but still he was obsessed in a similar way to the man Philip that Yalom described.

He forced his first wife Margareta to have sex with him every day, twice: early in the morning and a second time in the evening.

"I told you about this before we got married. I told you we would have sex every morning and evening and you agreed with that!" was the argument Jirka most often used when Margareta was reluctant to fulfill his demands. Jirka realized that he couldn't think about anything but sex and his sexual needs. The joke from his childhood came to his mind: Dezo (a young gypsy) was staring at Niagara Falls. A friend of his asks him, "Dezo what are you thinking about?" "About sex," Dezo answered. "Explain to me how this huge water connects your thinking with sex?!" his friend replies. "How, how. I don't know how! I am always thinking about sex! That's how it is connected, you delino (=you stupid man)".

The relief from the sex-possessed thoughts came only after Margareta agreed to have sex. Same as Philip, Jirka also enjoyed those short moments of calmness when his mind stopped to think how he should convince Margareta to have sex again. He loved and enjoyed those short relaxed moments, not thinking about his sexual appetite. They lasted a couple hours, half a day max. Soon after that his mind was again plotting how to convince Margareta to have sex again.

Margareta on the other hand wanted to have sex once or twice a week. If Jirka wouldn't agree, she threatened to divorce Jirka. Jirka withdrew his demands for sex every day and they made a deal to have sex every other day. If that didn't happen he got angry and did not try to hide his anger. Jirka didn't think that his sex obsession was the main reason for the divorce that followed two years into marriage. He thought the main reason was the fact that he was just a blue color worker and that Margareta wanted something more; someone more educated, a more intelligent partner than Jirka.

Ohh and how much Jirka blamed Jozef for his destiny; for the letters that he wrote to Margareta during their time in Hradec Kralove. Yes, he blamed Jozef for his first marriage fiasco. Jirka loved Margareta; she had a permanent place within him. She stayed in Jirka's mind even 20 years after they separated and each went their own way.

Jirka also recognized himself in Yalom's client Rebecca. He wanted to get Margareta out of his mind; he didn't even think this was something that could be achieved. But he followed what Rebecca had done. No, he didn't go to India to practice yoga with Himalayan monks. He focused on his breathing the way Yalom described in every one of his books that Jirka had read: keep focusing on the breath-in and breath-out for at least 15 minutes every day; when you don't give up you will feel on the inside of your nostrils that the temperature of the air that goes in is lower than the temperature of the air coming out. This makes sense as the body makes the air warmer when the air gets in; the trick is that you must learn to focus on your breathing to notice that. By daily focusing on simple breathing you do what Buddha recommends: "Do not dwell on the past, do not dream of the future, concentrate the mind on the present moment". If you have a goal it's easier to practice focusing, which is the same as meditation.

As with Rebecca, it worked with Jirka too. Jirka combined the focus on the breathing with his 'putting the sky inside of him' practice and after several months of practicing, the daily thoughts about Margareta dispersed. To feel the temperature difference of the air coming in to his body and air coming out at the beginning of this daily focus Jirka tried a small cheat; he put his palm next to his nostrils and could clearly fell the difference. *If I can feel that with the help of my palm, I must feel that without any object near my nostrils*, said Jirka to himself. He practiced focusing during his yoga time, with his legs out straight and his body folded forward, looking inward. He didn't mark the calendar when he started this kind of meditation but one day he realized that Margareta had relinquished completely from his daily thinking.

Discipline in thinking! What would that mean? Who would even think that the mind needed to be trained to think in disciplined way? His aunt Gertruda wouldn't comprehend that concept. There would be a small chance of convincing her that she would be better off if she would implement a disciplined way of thinking. Gertruda was never diagnosed with any mental disorder. Who knows how some psychiatrist would diagnose Gertruda's self-talking; what they would advise her to do?

Jirka now realized that he was often doing what he observed in his aunt's behavior. He wouldn't perform loud self talking; instead his performance took place inside of him; hidden in his inner world. Is self talking (hidden or open) one of the symptoms of schizophrenia? If so, isn't it the case that the seeds of schizophrenia are placed inside of each of us? It is there somewhere in everybody's mind; most of us simply don't know about it. How many times has someone prepared an answer for the question that the teacher asked at the front of the class before he/she raised their hand to let everybody know that he/she knows the answer (and repeated this answer just for himself several times)? How many times are questions prepared inside of one's mind; questions that could arise during an exam or interview and right after that prepared answers to the questions ready as well? A fellow goes for an important date, he wants to impress his date, he is driving the car and inside in his mind he is creating possible scenarios with the questions and answers so he is ready to impress when the real situation arises. Humans do that, they are preparing themselves for important meetings, some of them might continue doing that even if the event in the near future is not so important… and then one suddenly realizes that preparing the questions and smart answers to those questions is getting out of control, the way of thinking is in uncontrolled loops.

Jirka got afraid that this was exactly what was now going on inside of his mind. Uncontrolled loops of creating situations in which he trains his mind to perform the best possible way. Creates answers on most likely questions that he could encounter in a situation that could happen but in reality would never take place. Is this schizophrenia or just a "beautiful mind"? Doesn't matter what the name is. It is uncontrolled; it's creating chaos and is clouding clear thinking. How to stop it? Put the thinking under control; in other words train your mind in disciplined thinking. How? Put the sky inside of you.

Jirka had decided to try that: 'Put the sky inside of him' and was determined not to give up. He had now been trying to put an image of the sky inside him every night before he fell asleep. When he walked he closed his eyes, not entirely, just so he can barely see the sky, so the image of the sky gets into his memory. The loops of his imaginary thinking are not under his control yet; however the fruit of his effort is starting to show up. When he presses to get the picture of the sky to his mind during the day, when he forgets about his sky at night, the picture of the sky comes to his almost sleeping mind, it doesn't hold too long but it shows up by itself; a clear, blue vivid image of the sky.

The pure preparation of questions and answers doesn't make one schizoid. There must be some other ingredients. An N.V. Gogol quote about anger and rage came to Jirka's mind. He had read Gogol's quote in one of Levi's book and couldn't quite recall the words. He couldn't find Levi's *"The Art Being Yourself"* among other Levi's books. He did a quick internet search and found out that all Levis books were now downloadable for free. He downloaded the book and found the N.V. Gogol's quote there. He re-read the sentence again and again trying to remember that quote word for word: *"To win over rage is much harder for one who at the present moment doesn't even have an idea that this depravity exists, than to one who already found out that rage is residing in him. For that person it's much easier because he knows against what he must fight, who is the real enemy; he feels now that in critical cases or situations he must stand up, not against that particular case or situation, but against his own rage... then he for sure gets over his own rage and its source that triggered the rage would disappear."*

The Roman philosopher Seneca, advisor to Emperor Nero, came to Jirka's mind. He had read about his life just yesterday; what caught Jirka's attention was that it was Seneca who was among the first known philosophers to connect inner rage with mental degradation. The inner rage is that ingredient that fuels the cognitive system to run deeper and deeper towards the event horizon, which then takes the cognitive thinking to the forever-lost black hole. *Is it the rage and inner anger that assist the innocent question-answer scenarios that the mind is preparing for real life performance to convert into uncontrolled loops?* Jirka wondered. *Gogol's quote! I have to keep that in my mind forever. This is what I possess: the inner anger and inner rage!* Jirko was convinced he had found his main enemy and he must remove that devil from his life!

Acknowledging this depravity is the most important step to getting out of the Event Horizon. And it was working. Whenever Jirka noticed his reaction fueled by anger he started reminding himself *I have that inside of me, this is it, this is that rage...* and he did slow deep breath in even slower breath out. He did that again and again whenever he noticed the anger in his reaction.

How does the cognitive human system work? When a human being is born and starts to grow up his mind is in its pure ontology mode. Then the mind starts to build a system of values; observing what others do; listening to what parents and teachers emphasize to do; building good/bad values; moral/immoral values; slowly adding those values to the huge storage somewhere there in the mind's unconscious universe. Life goes on and real life situations bring a subjective system of values into the conflict with the real world; the human ego might be convinced that it was cheated, betrayed and victimized; it could react several ways, one of them could be a stream of self pity mixed with anger. Life goes on, the inner anger slowly grows and gets a peculiar, justified place inside of the mind.

Is this what happened when Jirka found out that Margareta was cheating on him with his very good friend? His heart started to pump when he opened the door to see them *en flagrante*. Is it possible to completely get over that kind of picture written inside of the mind? Divorce would not erase it. Divorce might add to the self pity stream called depression but would not get the picture out of the mind. The uncontrolled stream of self-pity takes its tolls, affects the memory, destroys the cognitive working system. One suddenly realizes that the world in which he had lived doesn't exist; everything the cognitive system created, the physical image of the world with its values, everything collapses, ceases to exist. The mind has self-built a defense system against the stream of depression; it doesn't let this stream run forever. Those self-built defense systems force the mind into longer hours of sleepiness; much more than 7-8 hours which would be typical sleeping time; after several months eventually one might be able to control the stream of depression and stop it. AT is a very big help with that.

Jirka now realized why Julo read Levi's books and why he read them as well. The human mind has no in-built mechanism for dealing with anger and inner rage – it must be controlled manually. Place the switch inside the mind and whenever there is an event that triggers inner anger turn that switch on! What needs to be done is to recognize that a typical reaction is there and choose to turn on a reminder: *I am possessing this anger, this is that anger that is killing me...* then the switch that recognizes the anger is turned on, take a deep breath in and hold it inside for two-three seconds and even slower breathe out; the anger is able to diminish even before it started.

As Jirka did more reading he thought about what other ingredients fueled a devious type of thinking. Prestige, a desire to show others how good you are, a craving to become famous. It starts in childhood; a creative mind is praised for its creativity and what a good feeling it is to be praised. What a good feeling it is to have fun with building your own cognitive system and express to others how smart the system is. That is the way it should be and should stay until one dies. What happens though is that showing others how smart and good one is becomes more important than the original fun and pleasure of the learning; what others say about us becomes more important.

Jirka observed in himself the truth of the claim that he learned decades ago: "the more you try to find out what other people are saying about you, the more your self-confidence decreases." and noticed a similarity in Schopenhauer's *"Parerga and Paralipomena"* quote that he read in one of Yalom's book. "The flower replied: You fool! Do you imagine I blossom in order to be seen? I blossom for my own sake because it pleases me, and not for the sake of others. My joy consists in my being and my blossoming."

Jirka sought to understand himself. He learned by reading, discovering himself by reading what others might already know, not about him but about other human beings who had done similar things.

He'd figured out several years ago that, yes, he was consciously and unconsciously trying to find what other people said about him. When Jirka got back from Hradec Kralove he decided to finish high school and get his high school diploma. He didn't stop there; he went on to get a college degree. He liked to hear praise from others, to hear how others held him up as an example because of what he had done, what he had achieved.

After he divorced Margareta and was depressed, he read Levi's books; the same books Julo read in Hradec Kralove. He practiced AT, learning to control each muscle whether sitting in the chair, or lying on the couch. He focused on the relaxation of each muscle, exactly the same way they had done in Hradec Kralove and it helped Jirka to conquer his depression.

Now he remembered Levi's words from 20 years ago, *"the more you try to find out what other people say about you, the more your self-confidence decreases."* He was amazed by the truth of this claim; however it didn't really stop his craving to be praised. He had to go through another 12 years of the 'miserable life' (as Arthur Schopenhauer described his life) until he read Yalom and David Mitchell; only after that did he realize that he possessed the craving for prestige and that was another ingredient that took him one step closer to the event horizon of his own black hole. He knew that he must get rid of that craving.

Was there any other ingredient? Sure: money. Money is a special type of ingredient. It works both ways: it can fuel the cognitive system towards the event horizon or help one to get out of it. One can either have no money, possess money or money can possess one.

Jirka never forgot Mr. Papandreaos, a relatively wealthy man and owner of a prosperous Greek restaurant. When Jirka came back to Prague from Hradec Kralove he worked for a small remodeling firm. He worked on a bathroom remodeling project in Mr. Papandreaos's condominium. Mrs. Papandreaos had good taste, designed and choose new tiles, new faucet, new medicine cabinet, new toilet; they were not too expensive but not cheap either. The bathroom turned to be very nice and elegant after the remodeling project was completed. When it was time to write the final check for the project, Mr. Papandreous started to cry and protested to Mrs. Papandreous.

"Look what you have done to me! Look how much money we have to pay! The bathroom was OK before; it was just your extravagance and look, now I have to pay for that!" Mr. Papandreous was serious, he really cried. Money got him totally! He forgot that money was there to make people happy; in this case to make his wife happy. They had enough money; the restaurant business was performing well and his business earned more than enough to pay for this nice remodeling project. Money owned Mr. Papandreous and he didn't want to give it up.

Did money own Jirka too? Partially, yes. He got so upset when he found a ticket behind his windshield for a parking violation. He had to hide his upset when Margareta bought new clothes. Yep, money possessed Jirka. How would he get rid of that weed? Jirka had practiced the acts of a kindhearted person. When he visited his extended family he pulled out his wallet and gave pocket money to his nephews and nieces (in the same way he received pocket money from his uncle when he was young boy or when as a soldier he came home for couple of days off). Though Jirka thought he should give them more than he did he knew it was better than nothing and believed it would affect them. Perhaps they would do something similar when their turn came.

In that way Jirka understood that it was not money itself that would get one away from the event horizon. Money is simply the tool. It was the power of giving that was the ingredient that helped one to navigate one away from the black hole.

Jirka's determination to *'put the sky inside of him'* started to show results. He noticed that early in the morning, when his brain was slowly coming out of its sleeping stage to consciousness, his mind displayed an image of blue sky. The sky picture lasted just a couple of seconds, but it was a huge encouragement to Jirka. He now understood why one of the practices of AT was focusing on any image, holding and image in the mind as long as possible. The practice helped tremendously to improve brain cognitive functions that assist focus, memory and space orientation.

Jirka adjusted his daily routine to include keeping an image he found in the gym in mind and found this much more beneficial. He loved to combine his workout with AT. For the first 20 minutes he did his yoga/stretching routine and the remaining 20 minutes he worked out with weights focusing on keeping the image in his mind. The more he focused, the higher probability that he would see sky in his mind during the morning waking hours.

All this progress was great but there was still something not right with Jirka's mood; he knew that he is still not completely in control of his inner world. He remembered reading in Levi's book, "you are what you eat". Jirka had been a vegetarian. He thought that by eliminating the meat from his diet it would help him to live a much healthier and thus smarter way of life. When he looked back at the decision he made more than 20 years ago (and which lasted for about 12 years) he realized that by eliminating meat he craved more for sweet, sugary types of food. He didn't realize that the absence of the meat, which he partially replaced by sweet stuff, could bring more harm than benefit.

Later in his life, during his event horizon experience, he became convinced that the elimination of the animal source of protein was one of the reasons that his brain and body was not producing enough S-adenosylmethionine (SAM-e). The source of energy that keeps everything going is called ATP (Adenosine Thriphospate). The SAM-e is produced from ATP and it is naturally occurring in almost every tissue and fluid in the body; it works with B-vitamins (B12, B9). Insufficient levels of B vitamins can cause a low level of SAM-e and vice versa; kind of a closed loop. If SAM-e is supplied externally (for example via pills) it has to have enough B vitamins in order to absorb that supplement into the body. On finding all this out, Jirko decided to take 200 mg of SAM-e twice a day together with B vitamins, magnesium, vitamin D, omega3 fish oil and Ginko.

Why magnesium? Magnesium is a mineral; our body might have about 25 grams of it, mainly in the bones. Magnesium can increase levels of energy and endurance, helps to treat attention disorder, migraine, heart diseases; it decreases pain in the joints. It does a lot of good stuff so it's important to have the right level in the body. Magnesium could be supplied by meat, legumes, vegetables – such as broccoli, squash, green leafy vegetables – seeds, nuts such as almonds, chocolate and hard water.

Why vitamin D? If one has a strict vegan diet he might have a deficiency of vitamin D because some of the best sources of that vitamin are animal meat, fish, eggs, cheese and milk. Deficiency can cause cardiovascular diseases, cognitive impairment, asthma in children, or cancer. Vitamin D is also called the sunshine vitamin; somehow the body can get more vitamin D if it is exposed to the sun. He knew then that he shouldn't shun the sun; too little could be as dangerous as too much.

Why fish oil? To join the trend for recommended healthy eating and perhaps prevent heart disease.

Why Gingko? Jirka read several studies regarding this interesting supplement. Gingko biloba is one of the oldest tree species found on this planet and its leaves have many benefits to supply the human body and mind. One study found that Gingko can treat blood disorders and memory issues. What they also found was that people who don't have memory problems don't really benefit from taking Gingko as a regular supplement; one becomes a genius by taking Gingko. But Gingko might help to treat dementia and improve memory in those who really suffer from memory problems. In other words, to help one who is at the event horizon to get out of the black hole.

Later Jirka added curcumin and cinnamon to his daily supplement. Curcumin is the principal curcuminoid of turmeric. The body won't digest curcumin properly without black pepper. Thus if curcumin is taken without black pepper its benefits (such as possible treatment for cancer, gastrointestinal diseases, or cognitive disorders) would not count much.

Cinnamon, referred in the Hebrew Bible as 'holy anointing oil' is often used as a spice. Cinnamon has history of use in traditional medicine but currently there is no evidence that it can actually treat any medical conditions. Still, it could have lot of health benefits, such as to better control the level of the sugar in the blood, increase sensitivity to the hormone insulin, and lower the risk of heart disease and the level of cholesterol.

Jirka did what he did about 20 years ago when he started his vegetarian diet and *'took the brick of this current wisdom and added it to the building of his own stupidity.'* What was the brick of wisdom now? Fat and animal protein; veggies and fruit, no wheat, no flour products and no sugar! No sugar, no sugar! Repeat one more time: no sugar! Levi warned about sugar; and every diet recommends less sugar. When one gets close to the event horizon, he knows why sugar can kill the same way as a drug addict knows that the particular drug he is taking is killing him.

Jirka also drank water, and lots of it. 80 percent of the brain is water after all. How much water? About two liters (1/2 of gallon) per day? No, coffee didn't count. Green tea? Yes, green tea with Gyokuro does. Gyokuro tea traditionally harvested in Japan, Jirka read, contained a variety of natural compounds from which the human body could benefit; for example gyoukuru can contribute to slowing down aging, to treating heart diseases, cancer, diabetes, and digestive disorders.

The final wisdom that Jirko considered very important was simply deep breathing. Jirka noticed that by paying attention to his breathing after a while he naturally started to breath the way he read in the yoga books: deep slow breath in (4 seconds); keep the breath in the lungs (2 seconds) and even slower breath out (6 seconds).

Jirka and Jozef 27 years later

Punto, Jirko's dog, was happily wiggling his tail. He knew he was going out for his regular afternoon walk and gladly expressed his happiness.

"OK, my friend, I will take you today on a special walk. We will go up on Golden Street (*Zlata ulicka*) and check which soldier is standing like steel at the entrance of Prague Castle," Jirko told Punto while putting a leash around him.

They went out and walked slowly. *The power is in peace and calmness* Jirko reminded himself and deeply, slowly breathed in the fresh spring air in and even slower let the breath go out his nose. He looked at the sky, clear, blue sky with a couple of white cloudlets. He closed his eyes to make sure he could see their image even when his eyes were closed, and reopened his eyes again. The white cloudlets were still there; their shape changed a little bit.

As usual there were a lot of tourists in the courtyard before the entrance of the castle. Jirko looked at a boy standing next to the gate-keeping soldier. *This boy is Jozef, thought Jirko, how did he never get older?* He then looked back to see who was taking a picture of the boy. *That is Jozef! And the young boy must be his son or nephew.*

Jirko walked close to the person holding the camera, he didn't want to embarrass himself by incorrectly identifying a person who he had not seen in 27 years.

Jozef looked at Jirko saying, "It's hard to believe. Jirko?"

"Yeah, it's me," said Jirko, grinning as he embraced Jozef, "and I bet that boy is your son."

"Yes it is. Ludvig, or Ludo, he prefers Ludo."

"Like father like son," said Jirko. "I can't believe it, what a coincidence to see you here."

"Perhaps it's not. I wanted to see you, Jirko, so perhaps telepathy is working. I haven't seen you for years. I thought it would be nice to see an old friend before he dies."

"You are not serious are you? Die? I am fifty-one! I am not planning to die!" Jirko said.

"Sorry. I didn't express myself correctly."

"Hey, no worries old man."

Tourists started to gather near the castle entrance. It was close to noon so the guard changing ceremony would start soon.

"I was planning to watch the ceremony," Jozef said, "are you in hurry?"

"No, I am not. All time belongs to me and it would be my pleasure to watch the ceremony with you and your son, if that is ok with you."

Jirka has changed, Jozef thought, *he would never use that kind of language 27 years ago.*

"Yes, let's watch it together."

They watched the guard ceremony with all its pomp and grandeur and when it ended Jozef said, "Jirko, my son has his own program for the afternoon. I was planning to walk in the old town this afternoon, enjoying the good weather…"

"Punto and I will walk with you then…"

"Perfect! So he is Punto. Hi Punto! How if life treating you?"

"I bet better than me and you," smiled Jirko, "so, why you didn't come for Julo's funeral?"

"I couldn't, I was in hospital. I fell off the roof when I was cleaning gutters. I was lucky, nothing serious happened to me, just a small concussion, nothing broken. God likes me I guess. I heard it was a heart-breaking funeral."

"Yes it was. I couldn't hide my tears looking at Kamilka and Verunka. Jan, his close friend, told me how it happened."

"How did he know?"

"Julo's wife told him. She said she saw how Julo opened the kitchen window, he went then to the girls' bedroom for a second or two then came to her, gave her hug from the back, said nothing, turned away and started to sprint towards the window and then jumped through…" after a short pause Jirka continued, "Jan had been working together with Julo for the previous two years. Julo never told him anything. Jan was not aware that Julo could do what he did and blamed Julo for not mentioning anything, for not talking to him."

"And you, do you know why?" asked Jozef.

"No. I think Julo was good at hiding his troubled soul. Even Kristina, Julo's wife, didn't know why Julo did it. She blamed herself, at least partially. I told her not to do that, not to blame herself."

"What will happen to Kamilka and Verunka?"

"I don't know. I think Julo's older brother will take custody. I heard Kristina doesn't want to be with them; she wants to move away without Julo's children."

"Sad. Too sad. Last time I saw Julo was at my mom's funeral. I noticed pain in his eyes and from time to time it seemed as if he would be lost somewhere inside of himself. What do you think, Jirka? Why he didn't want to live?"

"Hmm. We can just speculate…"

Jirka and Jozef walked quietly for several minutes before Jirka broke the silence.

"You know what, Jozef? I think Julo got himself to the event horizon and he was not able to get out of it; rather than to be pulled inside to his black hole he decided to end his life."

Jozef looked at Jirko, didn't say anything for a while, not sure how to react. Was Jirko losing his mind or was there some hidden inappropriate joke?

"I got myself close to the event horizon. I don't wish anybody to get there," Jirko continued, "When you are getting there your cognitive thinking slowly stops working, closer to the event horizon thinking worsens, memory stops functioning, creating coherent sentences becomes a problem, words that come to mind lose their meaning and you are not sure whether what you are saying makes sense, your orientation becomes nonsense, and you are not sure whether you will be able to find your way to your destination, if you remember what that destination is."

Jozef realized that Jirka was not talking nonsense; he saw that he was talking about some serious things that happened to him. He was not sure how to encourage him to continue so he didn't say anything, which was all the encouragement for Jirka needed.

"You realize that something bad is coming to you; you feel that you might not be able to get out of it, you are not losing hope yet your desperation increases in geometrical order."

Jozef saw Jirka's deep breath in and slow breath out; he did that several times and then continued.

"Your mind, your cognitive thinking is slowly stopping to be cognitive, the fog inside of your mind is replacing clear thinking, it is accompanied by cicada-like humming; you try to read a book but you can't get a meaning of its plot, you are forgetting the names of your friends, short term memory isn't working, you can't remember things that you have done so many times, like you can't remember the password that you have been entering daily into your email account for the past two years; or in the morning you take vitamins from three bottles and after a minute or two you can't remember whether you took them or not... You know you are there; Alzheimer's or schizophrenia fits what you are experiencing inside of you... you know what would follow if you don't do anything... the black hole... the irreversible fall into a total dementia, a similar thing that happened to Nietzsche: 10 years of living dead."

"Jirka, this sounds awful," Jozef interrupted Jirka's monolog, "that you personally would have been experiencing this ugly stuff. I look at you and, sorry to say that, but I don't see a person with Alzheimer's or schizophrenia," Jozef smiled at Jirka in a similar way to how Jirka smiled at Jozef all those 27 years ago.

"Thank you..." said Jirka.

"Thank you for what?"

"For the compliment... Jozef, those things don't happen suddenly within a week or two, not even by month or two. They slowly get inside of you, year by year... you are lucky if you realize soon enough you've got it and you figure out how to get out of that spiral thinking that got you there..."

"I admit I don't know what you are talking about," said Jozef, shaking his head a little.

"Did you read Levi's books that Julo brought with him to Hradec Kralove?"

"Which books? If I remember correctly, Julo brought several books with him."

"The Art to Being Yourself? The Art to Being Somebody Else? The Art of Communications?" Jozef asked.

"I thought '*The Art to Being Somebody Else*' and '*The Art of Communication*' were the same book. The first is the translation into Slovak and the second is translated into Czech. I believe the third book Julo brought with him was '*The Formula of Personality*'. I read all three of them. It was so many years ago. I vaguely remembered the essence of the books."

"I re-read them a few years ago when I knew I had to do something not to fall into my own black hole," said Jirka.

"And you think that you have succeeded?" Jozef filled the short pause in Jirka's monolog.

"Sometimes I think I have, many times I think I am still too close to the event horizon. I know one thing; the course I have adopted is correct."

"What course?" asked Jozef.

"I knew I must to do something when I was heading towards the event horizon; somewhere from inside of me popped up the sentence that I read in Levi's book back in our Hradec Kralove era: *'put the sky inside of you.'* Deeply inside me I believed that putting the sky inside of me would save me. I made this my inside priority. I have decided to *'put the sky inside of me.'* No matter what it takes to do that. I have been practicing it for a few years now. I think I am starting to understand how the cognitive system in the human mind works. If the mind gets into the schizophrenic loop mode it suppresses image creating. You need to build a switch inside of your mind; when you notice the schizophrenic loops taking its place you just remind yourself *'not in the past, not in the future, leaves current moments'* deep breath in, slow breath out, look at the sky and try to copy the image of the sky into your mind. After a while you realize that this is how you lived when you were a kid, in ontology mode. The uncontrolled schizophrenic loops become controlled, they slowly disappear and the picture-creating mode takes place in your cognitive thinking. When I go to sleep I remind myself to see the sky image early in the morning before my mind wakes up. I look forward to those morning hours when my slowly comes out of full sleeping mode to semi-sleeping mode. I know I am waking up and in that moment the image of the sky comes to display; a blue sky with a few white clouds. I can keep that image for a while now. It looks like the longer I can keep the sky image, the further away I am from the event horizon..."

He paused, his voice raw and authentic.

"And how do you know you are out of event horizon?" Jozef asked quietly.

"When you are there the fear accompanies you; from time to time fear takes you over and you wonder if you'll ever get out this. I'll tell you what happened to me. It was about two and half years of daily practice of my own thirty minutes yoga type of stretching and meditation. It's doesn't really matter what kind of yoga postures you practice, what is important that you do that daily. I do that every morning right after I wake up; thirty minutes every morning and then thirty minutes every afternoon. People who have experienced an earthquake might know what I am going to describe. It was around 3 or 4 am. Something woke me up and I started to feel a vibration like a space rocket shaking as it is launching. The shaking was inside of my head, my consciousness became part of a stone avalanche, there was a loud cracking noise accompanied by lightning. I couldn't do anything; I understood what is going on and understood that my consciousness could go now either way: back to the black hole or out of the event horizon to join the normal world as you and I think the normal world should look like. This lasted for a couple of seconds; perhaps the same way as Big Bang lasted when the Universe as we know it was created in couple of seconds about fourteen billion years ago. The mind-quake stopped; right after that my mind relaxed for a tenth of a second and displayed gorgeous blue skies. When I saw the blue skies I knew I was ok now. The journey out of the event horizon was completed. I was heading out of there and I can't and don't want to go back there. I was thinking again and again about those couple of seconds that I experienced and tried to understand whether this was really what my mind went through when it's cognitive system was pushed to normality or it was just my clever dream maker that created this sci-fi like movie for me so I could convince myself that all is ok now and I don't have to be worried that I will end up my journey on this world as my aunt Gertruda did…"

"Hmm interesting," Jozef broke the short silence after Jirka stopped his monolog, "I don't know what to say… I was not expecting our conversation would turn this way. So you think that if Julo did what you are describing, trying to put the sky inside him, it would have saved his life?"

"I can't answer that. I would definitely have suggested him to try it. What Levi said about understanding yourself is true: you can't know and understand yourself until you change yourself. You have to really mean it. You have to stop blaming. I mean blaming somebody else or a group of people or even the particular event for whatever happens to you. You can't move forward, or should I say backward from the black hole, if you don't adopt this main axiom: no blaming! Inner anger must stop; self-pity must stop. If you notice that you are nervously trying to do something in a hurry, remind yourself that 'power is in peace and calmness'; if you notice that your reaction is triggering inner anger, remind yourself *'it is inside of me'* and take a deep breath. I've come to realize that Gogol's claim is correct: you win, the source of the anger disappears and you are capable of reacting with a smile, a true smile and instead of an angry reaction you can create a pleasant atmosphere. The hardest part is to get rid of craving to be recognized as the good one, to be praised, to become famous and learn to do things for the pleasure, just for the pleasure, just for the fun of doing it; not to hear somebody say you are good. Do something for somebody else without any expectation of getting anything back. It's not easy to do that: give something for free as clearly as fresh snow on the Himalaya mountains, with no contamination. It is the power of giving, not with force but easy, steady and without expectations…"

"You sound like ancient sage," Jozef jumped in with a smile in the short silence, "I know what you are saying is true and I like to hear that. I am just surprised. You have changed so much it's hard for me to believe that it is you: the Jirka that I met in Hradec Kralove."

"I have changed. I told you so. I had to." Jirka said a little solemnly.

"I understand; life brings you into the situations in which you must act."

"I am really glad I could see you again, Jozef. I had blamed you for my destiny but not anymore. I adopted Nietzsche's claim: 'what doesn't kill me, makes me stronger.' My past life didn't kill me. I think it made me stronger."

"Same here, Jirko. Before we go, what would be the most important thing you would advise Julo to do before he jumped out of his apartment window?"

"Hmm, I think I would ask him to honestly say to himself whether there was blame inside of him; blame that he considered justified. Acknowledging the existence of blame inside is perhaps the most important thing. Then stopping blaming somebody else for something that happened in the distant past is much easier… I would say to him to let those past events go away; let them disappear… If you can feel the air when you deeply breathe in and feel the warmer air when you breathe out, then nothing is lost. Look at the sky and try, just try, to put it inside of you…"

About the Author

Milos Toth is a graduate of George Washington University in artificial intelligence and a graduate of Technical University of Kosice, Slovakia, in robotics. He was born in Slovakia; for the past twenty-seven years, he has been living in Chevy Chase, Maryland.

Printed in the United States
By Bookmasters